FALLING WITH YOU

A FRACTURED CONNECTIONS NOVEL

CARRIE ANN RYAN

Falling With You
A Fractured Connections Novel
By: Carrie Ann Ryan
© 2019 Carrie Ann Ryan
ISBN: 978-1-947007-55-0

Cover Art by Charity Hendry
Photograph by Sara Eirew

For more information, please join Carrie Ann Ryan's MAILING LIST.
To interact with Carrie Ann Ryan, you can join her FAN CLUB

DEDICATION

To Liz.
Thanks for believing and trusting

FALLING WITH YOU

The day I lost my best friend was the day I realized that I'd been living in the past. I've tried to find a way to heal, to mend that break. Somehow, I came through it partially whole. But I know I couldn't have done that without Aiden Connolly.

The problem is, he once loved my best friend. And now she's gone, and I refuse to be in that shadow, or worse, a replacement for someone we both loved.

I left them all behind.

My brother.

My family.

My best friend.

And her.

Only Sienna Knight doesn't realize what she means to me. But before I can make sure she knows, I need to figure out exactly what that is.

CHAPTER ONE

Sometimes life knocks you down. Getting back up seems like something just for the movies.

-Sienna, age 14.

SIENNA

I HAD A HEADACHE, and I didn't think having another drink was going to help. Was it going to stop me, though? No. Was the fact that I needed to drive home going to stop me?

Totally.

I'd only had one glass of wine, but that would have to be enough for me. Because although I loved drinking at my friends' bar, I wasn't going to be an idiot about it.

Oh, I could be an idiot about many things, but not when it came to the amount of wine I had before I got into my car.

But none of these precautions actually helped my headache.

I looked over at my sister, Violet, and held back a cringe. I didn't really have any room to comment on headaches, considering that Violet got migraines almost constantly, and they sometimes came out of nowhere and left her in debilitating pain.

I didn't have that kind of pain. I just had a stress headache from two long days at work and trying not to think about everything that I was thinking about.

But I was fine. Everything was fine. I would just go home and forget that I was stressed about my job, that I was still missing my best friend, and the fact that I had a crush on the guy currently sitting next to me.

A guy I really shouldn't have a crush on.

Because I'd had that crush for a decade now.

A freaking *decade*. And he hadn't even been in my life for some of the years in the middle. Plus, he had been dating my friend at the beginning.

I had no right to have a crush on Aiden Connolly.

But it was really hard not to when he kept smirking, glowering, glaring, or sometimes even smiling.

Not that he smiled often, but I still had that crush even when he didn't.

It was a no good, terrible, very bad crush.

No wonder I had a headache.

Because Aiden always gave me a headache.

No, *thinking* about him gave me the headache.

And despite how hard I tried not to do it, I tended to think about Aiden more than I should. That meant a lot of stress, a lot of headaches, and a lot of just feeling like I was making one wrong decision after another.

"What's wrong?" Harmony asked, leaning into me on my other side.

We were sitting at one of the round tables in the corner at the Connolly Brewery. Our friends from back in our school days—now our friends again—owned the place. It used to be owned by Jack and Rose Connolly before they passed away, and then had been passed down to their three kids.

Cameron, Brendon, and Aiden were foster brothers, although Aiden and Cameron were actually twins who had then been adopted into the family. There was a fourth brother now, the half-brother to Cameron and Aiden, but they were all still Connollys, if not by blood or name then by choice.

The place had almost gone bankrupt a few months ago, but the three brothers had come together to find a way to make it work, and now it thrived.

That meant it was very busy in the place, and even though it was their night off, all three men were constantly getting up to help. Even Violet and Harmony pitched in, and considering that Violet was dating Cameron, and Harmony was dating Brendon, it made sense that they wanted to help their men.

I wasn't dating any of the Connollys. No, not even Aiden. Or even their younger—*very* younger—brother, Dillon.

So, since I was not dating any of them, that meant if I tried to help, they all just gave me weird looks.

Not that I wasn't actually helpful, but because it naturally meant that I usually ended up having to help Aiden because of the logical pairing.

And the two of us fought. A lot.

I had no idea why, but he just got under my skin. I might have a huge crush on him, but that didn't mean he didn't annoy me.

And he annoyed me so much.

"Sienna?"

I shook my head and looked over at Harmony. "I'm fine. Just a little headache."

"I'm sorry, is there anything I can do?" Harmony asked, her voice soft.

Harmony was the nicest of us all. She had been through hell and back and had come out stronger for it, even though I would never say that to her. She hated the word *strong,* and considering that it came to my mind often when I thought about her, I could see why she hated it. She had lost her husband a couple of years ago and had had to rebuild her life. And then we'd all lost our best friend, Allison, after she had taken her own life.

So, we'd all gone through hell, but Harmony had been through more. But now, she was smiling more, and even though I thought she was slightly delicate, she was always sweet and amazing.

That probably had to do with the fact that the man she'd fallen in love with sat on her other side. Brendon Connolly. Our friend, and now Harmony's other half.

The two of them had recently started dating, and I knew it was love and all the lovely magic that happened at the beginning of relationships.

I knew I probably sounded a bit cynical with that, but it was actually true, and I had a feeling that these two would go all the way. Marriage, maybe even babies. The same with Cameron and Violet.

That left me alone. Along with Aiden. But that was *not* going to happen.

Of course, there was some new blood in the water now, too—and no, not the eighteen-year-old Dillon.

The bartender Beckham had joined our group, even though he was working tonight and not sitting at our table. He was one sexy, bearded man, and I knew he had given me a few looks.

But for some reason, he didn't put on any moves, and because I didn't want things to get awkward, especially considering all of the connections we had with each other, I didn't put any moves on him either.

And that was just fine, because I had a feeling his eyes were for someone else.

But that person wasn't with us tonight either.

"Sienna? Are you okay?"

I tossed back the last of my water and nodded. "I'm fine, just lost in my head. And because of that, I think I should head home. I have an early day tomorrow, and I'm just not feeling it. You know?"

Harmony reached out and gripped my hand. "If you're sure. We're here if you need us."

"I'm fine. Seriously. Nothing's wrong. I'm just a little out of sorts tonight. Maybe a long bath and a good book before I go to bed will help. You know?"

"That sounds wonderful," Harmony said, smiling.

"Did someone say bath?" Brendon asked, his voice a

little low and too growly for me. He kissed Harmony's neck, and I rolled my eyes.

"Okay, you two. Paws off each other while I say goodbye to everyone."

"Oh? You're leaving?" Violet asked as she stood up with me.

"Are you sure? Are you feeling okay?"

"I'm fine. I just explained to Harmony that I have an early morning. You guys have fun tonight because you all deserve it. I deserve a nice warm bath."

"Okay, text me when you get home so I know you're safe." Violet kissed my cheek and gave me a hug, and then I went through and hugged all of the others, saying my goodbyes. I ended up at Aiden's side, and he just raised a brow at me.

"Do you want a hug, too, Connolly?"

"I'm sure you'll give me one, but I need to head out too since I'm not actually working tonight, and sitting here and trying not to micromanage the kitchen is starting to get under my skin."

Aiden was possibly one of the best chefs I'd ever met. I'd had some amazingly prepared food in my time, but Aiden was the best. He had left his job at a Michelin-starred restaurant to come work at the bar.

I knew it might seem like a step down for some, but

Aiden had been very clear in saying that he hadn't liked his other place. That he wouldn't have made it far there because of who owned the restaurant and who the other sous chefs were. Apparently, everybody at that place preferred hiring cousins and sons rather than chefs with any actual talent.

So, he was sprucing up the brewery and making the place a little classier than it had been.

I was just fine with that because it meant I got to taste all the good things.

Not that I'd tell Aiden that he was amazing. That might just give his ego a little bit too much of a boost. And he did not need help with his ego.

"Aw, did the big, bad Aiden have a bad day? Was he yelling at all his poor little people?"

"Why do you have to sing-song when you ask that? I just can't with you." He shook his head and then handed me my purse. "Let's go."

"I can walk to my car just fine. It's not like there aren't lights everywhere."

"Yeah, you can. But I'm going the same way. So, let's just get this over with."

"Oh, my hero. Whatever shall I do without you?"

He just grunted something under his breath, and I had a feeling it wasn't anything nice. But it didn't really matter what it was. I was heading out the door, and I was going to get over my crush.

Because having a crush on Aiden Connolly had done nothing for me over the past decade. And keeping with it was only going to make things worse.

We had made it just around the corner when Aiden cursed under his breath.

"What's wrong?"

"I forgot my phone. Do you want to come back with me?"

"Not particularly. I've probably walked this street over a hundred times on my own. I'll be fine."

"I'd rather not leave you alone," Aiden growled.

"I have my little cat ears that I can stab someone with." I took out my keys and made a little punching motion with the keychain's sharp, pointy ears.

"You look adorable."

"You said that so truthfully, too. I totally believe you."

"Come on, Sienna. Walk back with me."

"I'm tired, Aiden. I'll be fine. Go, get your phone. I'm going to head home. I've worked later hours before, and the place where my job is at is in an actual bad part of the city. We're not exactly there now."

"Just don't be stupid, short stack," Aiden growled and then turned on his heel, jogging towards the bar.

Knowing him, he would probably run there, get his phone, then sprint back so he could walk with me the last bit of the way. I didn't mind him being protective, it was just when he got overly so that it got weird.

But I wasn't going to be stupid. So, I made sure my crossbody bag was secure, my little cat ears were firmly on my fingers, ready to punch out, and I had my phone in my other hand, queued to call 911 just in case.

You couldn't be too careful when it came to being a woman alone, even if it wasn't quite dark out yet.

I had just turned right when the first hand grabbed me.

At first, I thought it was Aiden, trying to teach me a lesson or something, so I didn't punch out when I should have.

And I really should have.

One hand grabbed my neck, the other pulled on my hair.

And when the hot, putrid breath slid across my neck, I knew it wasn't Aiden.

"What?" I asked, trying to get words out. Suddenly, another hand was on my neck, and I knew there was more than one man.

And those hands were big, rough, and callused.

They smelled, they were dirty, and they were on me. Someone pushed me into the brick wall of the alley, and I screamed. Only no sound really came out because there was still a hand over my mouth.

Tears formed in my eyes at the pain as my cheek scraped the brick, but I couldn't freak out, I had to get out of this. Hadn't I just told Aiden that I was safe?

I tried to reach for my phone, but the guy took it and tossed it down the alley, the crunching sound echoing in my head.

"Bitch. Give me all your money."

But he was tugging at my purse, hard enough that the strap dug into my shoulder. I knew it would leave a bruise. I kicked out, trying to remember what I had learned from that week of self-defense classes I had taken.

They hadn't been enough. I had been so sure that I was safe, that I was making mistake after mistake now that I wasn't.

There were three of them with grabby hands tugging on my coat, my purse. They weren't touching me anywhere else, they were being very careful not to. Maybe I was just blocking it all out.

I fought back, kicking and trying to scratch them. But one man had his hand firmly around my wrist, squeezing so hard I thought he might break it. My hand opened, my keys fell out, and the cat ears that were supposed to save me did nothing.

And then the men were off me, and I could breathe again.

I hit the ground, my knees radiating sharp pain.

And Aiden was there, punching, kicking, using his fists all on one man's face.

I tried to get to my feet, but I was achy, and my head felt light.

I hadn't even realized that the man's hand had been so tight around my throat earlier, squeezing. I'd been so far in my head, trying to figure a way out, that I hadn't realized I hadn't been breathing.

And then there was the sound of feet against pavement as the three men ran, and Aiden was on the ground next to me, holding me.

"Sienna? Sienna? Talk to me. What's wrong? What hurts? God, baby. I'm so sorry."

I was on his lap, and he was holding me, one hand cupping my face, the other held close to his body. I looked down and instantly knew something was wrong.

Aiden, the talented and amazing chef, the one that used his hands to create masterpieces, was holding his hand in such a way that I had a feeling it was broken.

Broken on someone's face. To protect me.

And that was my fault. He was hurt. All because I had told him to go away. Because I'd thought I was strong enough.

Because I'd thought I could handle it on my own.

But obviously, I couldn't.

"Sienna?"

"I tr—I—" I tried to get out words, but I couldn't, so Aiden just kissed my temple and held me close, and I tried not to lean into him, tried not to do anything. Because I didn't want him to be hurt again.

It was my fault that he was hurt, my fault for everything.

I didn't even realize I was shaking until he was whispering soft, soothing things into my ear that I couldn't decipher.

"It's okay, I called the cops, they're coming. They're coming, Sienna. Just hold onto me. You're going to be fine."

"Sorry," I whispered, but my voice was a ragged exhale.

He cursed under his breath, and I had no idea what happened next. I didn't pass out, I was awake, but everything just happened so quickly. The cops were suddenly there, sirens blazing. People were running, shouting. I didn't know what was wrong. I didn't know anything.

I just found myself being pulled from Aiden's arms, his growl of a voice telling them what he had seen.

He gave his statement, and then there were paramedics, taking care of us both.

I still had my purse on, but my keys were on the ground, and my phone was somewhere down the alley.

I think I told them that, but I don't really remember.

I blinked a few times, and then I was in the ER, sitting on the edge of one of those beds.

My feet dangled, and I wondered why. Shouldn't I be lying back? Shouldn't I be settled, trying to get better?

Why was I sitting?

"Miss Knight? I need you to answer a few questions, okay?"

The female doctor was sweet, her voice soft. Caring. And I needed that. I didn't know why, but I needed that.

"They didn't touch me," I said quickly. Because I knew that look in her eyes, I knew what she was asking. "They didn't touch me like that. They just put their hands on my wrist and my neck, and they tried to get my purse. But they didn't touch me."

They didn't do what would've been the worst thing that any woman could deal with.

And I was lucky. I might be bruised, I might be broken, but I was lucky.

"Okay, we're just going to finish checking you over, okay? And the cops are here, and they're going to want to hear what you have to say. Your family's here, too."

I blinked again, trying to get my thoughts in order. I was fine. I was just fine. Just a little banged up. And once I got through the shock, I would be fine.

It could've been worse. It could've been *so* much worse.

And then I thought of Aiden.

"Aiden? Is he okay?" I knew my words were fast, my voice a little high. But he needed to be okay.

"The man who came in with you? He's with another doctor right now. His family's here, as well, and it seems that you all know each other. Once I'm allowed to give you his status, I will. But first, let's just worry about you, okay?"

"He needs that hand. He needs to be okay. He's a really great chef. You would love the Connolly Brewery. They're really great. I mean, they used to be great before, but now they're even better because the brothers are working together, you know? And I really think that you should try it. Aiden does this thing with tapas. He makes it really fancy, even though it's not too fancy. So, it's not like pretentious or anything. I really think you'd like it."

I knew I was rambling, and the doctor just nodded and then started to check me over.

And then Harmony and Violet were there, with Meadow right on their tail.

Meadow hadn't been out with us, but here she was, our new friend, our new fourth.

And then I could breathe again. Because I wasn't alone. But I had to make sure that Aiden was okay.

Aiden had to be okay.

The doctor finished with me, and it turned out I only

had a few bruises and scrapes. I would be fine and could go home soon.

I went through my statement and told the cops everything I could remember. They had found my phone, though the glass was shattered. They had found my keys and had handed them over.

I had been mugged, and yet I had everything that I'd had before.

Maybe.

"Okay, you're going to come home with me, okay," Violet said, her voice soft.

"I just want to go home," I whispered. "The cats."

Violet just smiled. "Meadow's going to take care of your cats for you. And Beckham's going to go with her so she's not alone. No one's going to be alone tonight. You're going to come home with me. I'm going to tuck you in and love you and do my best not to freak out. Because if I freak out, then Mace and Adrienne will be right here. You know our big brother tried to get in that car and drive up here. But I wouldn't let him. He will be here tomorrow, though, and we can't stop that. But tonight, you're coming home with me. Okay?"

Violet was talking very calmly, very precisely, and I just nodded. I didn't want to be alone, not really. But my babies were at the house. Though if Meadow and

Beckham were going to take care of them, then that would be okay.

"What about Aiden?"

Violet and Harmony and Meadow all shared a look, and they stiffened.

"What about Aiden?" I repeated.

"The guys are with him now. He's going to go home a bit later than you. But we can wait if you'd like. He broke his hand. It's not a bad break, but it's enough that it's going to be in a cast for a few weeks."

Tears filled my eyes, and I started shaking.

"But he needs to work. How can he do that?"

"They're going to figure it out. And Dillon is ready to step in. We're all going to be fine. You just need to worry about yourself for now. Aiden will be just fine." I looked at Harmony and nodded, but I couldn't really focus.

Because while I might be bruised and still in shock, I wasn't the one going home in a cast.

Aiden was the one hurt. All because I thought I could take care of myself.

I had been wrong.

And the guy I'd had a crush on for so long, the man that I secretly loved even though I shouldn't, had been hurt because of me.

If I hadn't had my pride, he would be fine.

It was all my fault.

CHAPTER TWO

AIDEN

I KNEW I HAD A TEMPER, but damn, this week? I felt like my rage was out of control.

And there was nothing I could do about it.

My hand hurt, my head hurt, and I was just so pissed off at the world, that it felt like nothing I did was the right thing.

It had been four days since I had seen Sienna. Four days since I had seen her pinned against that wall, fighting with everything she had, but both of us afraid that it wouldn't be enough.

I had been so damn scared.

Was *still* scared. I hadn't been just scared in that moment though, I had been angry as all hell that someone dared to touch her. They'd made her feel unsafe. They'd tried to steal her purse, her phone, and God knew what else. They probably made her doubt herself, and that killed me. Because Sienna *never* doubted herself. She was the most confident woman I knew. So much so that she annoyed the hell out of me sometimes because we butted heads over it. Over her. Over me. Over all of it. But now, she was hurt, and there wasn't a damn thing I could do about it.

I was scared right at this very moment just thinking about it.

And so angry.

I hadn't seen Sienna since that night. I hadn't talked to her. Held her. I hadn't done a damn thing.

That worried me more than it probably should have. Or maybe not enough.

Did she blame me?

Maybe she should. Because I hadn't been there. I had left her alone. When I voiced my concern, she had waved me off, and I left her.

I should have stayed.

Maybe if I had stayed, she wouldn't have been hurt.

Maybe if I had stayed, she wouldn't have been scared.

Maybe if I had stayed, I wouldn't have broken my fucking hand.

Maybe if I had stayed, I wouldn't be lost as to what the hell I was going to do.

Because I truly had no idea what the fuck to do.

I sat in my house, in the dark even though it was light outside. I just hadn't opened my blinds, and I didn't really want to.

I wasn't allowed to work yet, even to stand in the kitchen and order people around.

The doctors said that I might be able to soon, but my brothers told me I needed to stay at home. I needed to rest. I needed to get to a hundred percent mentally before I could step foot in that kitchen and try to figure out what the fuck I was going to do.

For all I knew, the whole place that I had helped rebuild was just going down in flames.

Yeah, I might be a little egocentric, but I wasn't so much so that I thought that no one could run things without me. But, still. I was the one who had made the menu. I was the one who had taught everyone in that kitchen what they needed to do.

I was the one who had fired a couple of people who didn't like the change and wanted to do things the way they had been.

The thing was, they hadn't really been doing too good of a job under Jack. But my dad had wanted to keep them on because he had a hard time firing people.

He hadn't had such a hard time when I was younger, but as he'd gotten older, after he had lost Rose, he'd had a harder time keeping the good people on staff and not firing those who didn't need to be there.

Maybe it was sentiment, perhaps he just hadn't cared anymore after losing his wife.

My mom.

I didn't know what Jack had been thinking those months, but the almost failing of the bar wasn't just on him. It was on the whole lot of us, and the fact that we Connollys hadn't been there to help him. I had spent the last few months changing my life, completely putting myself into the place that had been my father's, my mother's, my family's. And now I wasn't there to see it through.

Because I'd broken my fist on some fucker's face.

Yeah, I was pissed off. But maybe it was what I deserved.

Regardless, Sienna hadn't deserved any of that.

And I hadn't spoken to her since the incident.

Oh, I wanted to. I wanted to make sure that she was okay, but all I had been able to do was look at her in the distance when she passed me in the emergency room and nodded at me.

She nodded at me, even though she wouldn't say a word.

She had been pale, her eyes wide, a little glassy.

I had never seen Sienna like that.

She was seriously one of the strongest, bravest people I had ever met in my life, and she was always in your face —loud, happy, and helpful.

She was like that Pinkie, the pink unicorn that bounced around on that little pony show that my ex-girlfriend had made me watch at one point. The fact that I was now worried that maybe Sienna wasn't a unicorn, but maybe just a regular pony told me that the pain meds might be making me a little off right then.

But that was life.

Sienna wouldn't talk to me. I had texted her once, and she hadn't texted back.

Maybe she had been sleeping, or perhaps she couldn't deal with me.

Nobody wanted to deal with me.

I was a grumpy asshole. I was proud of that usually, but now, I didn't know what to do.

Because Sienna was hurt. Yeah, so was I, but she had been hurt because I hadn't been there.

And I would kill the motherfucker who did it.

My doorbell rang, and I narrowed my eyes at it, annoyed at the damn door and anyone who would be at my house.

How could I brood and growl alone in the dark if someone was at my place?

Maybe I should leave the house. You know, cook and go to my place of business and actually do something productive rather than just sitting here wondering if I was going to waste away along with my accomplishments.

I wasn't even a damn sous chef anymore. I wasn't working at a Michelin-starred restaurant and being the best I could possibly be.

I was working at a damn bar, though one I was proud of.

But I wasn't really working at all right now, was I?

I wasn't doing anything.

The key in the lock turned, and Brendon and Cameron walked in, Dillon following closely behind them.

"I gave you that key for emergencies, assholes," I muttered under my breath, leaning back into the cushions of the couch.

Cameron flipped me off and closed the door behind him, while Dillon stuffed his hands into his pockets.

Brendon just shook his head. "Dear God, have you even showered today?"

I held up my wrist that was still in the cast. "Kind of hard to shower with this. So, why don't you just fuck off?"

"Wow, aren't you in a good mood?"

"I don't know," Cameron said, talking to Dillon and Brendon and ignoring me, "it sounds about the same type of mood that he's usually in. Maybe with a little more grime. God, you stink."

"I do not stink. I showered earlier. So, everyone just shut the fuck up." *At least I put on pants*, I thought to myself. Pants were good.

Pants were a sign of the sane.

No, not really. I was officially losing my damn mind.

"Well, if you say you're clean, I'm going to call you a liar," Cameron said quickly. "But, we're just here to check on you."

"I don't need a bunch of mother hens checking on me. I'm fine."

Dillon came up and sat on the other end of the couch and just stared. "Really, Aiden?"

I looked at my youngest brother and narrowed my eyes. I didn't know Dillon as well as I knew my other brothers, but then again, Dillon had just entered my life.

I hadn't known he even existed, not until he'd shown up for Jack's funeral with Cameron.

He was my half-brother, we shared a mother. When Cameron and I were younger, our mom hadn't been the best mother, and our dad had been long out of the picture. She had lost custody of us, and the foster system had split us up.

I hadn't even seen my own twin for a couple of years when we were kids until Jack and Rose ended up taking

24

us in, along with Brendon. So, Brendon, Cameron, and I had ended up growing up as brothers, and eventually, were adopted into the Connolly family.

Dillon however, was a few years younger than us and ended up staying with our mom.

Our biological mom that is.

When the piece of trash that called herself our mother called Cameron for help, which we later found out was because she was about to lose custody of Dillon, Cameron had gone to California, and I had been a douche about it.

I could admit that now. I had been a horrible human being. And I would regret that 'til the end of my days.

We hadn't known exactly why our birth mom needed us at the time, only that she'd said she needed us there. I assumed it had been for money or drugs or for something else I didn't want to deal with. But Cameron had the softer heart, so Cameron had gone, and found out about Dillon.

And I had felt like I lost my twin. I felt betrayed. As if everything we had worked for to make our new family wasn't worth it. As if Cameron didn't want any of it.

And so, I'd stayed. I left my brother to deal with whatever the woman wanted. And when Cameron had tried to contact Brendon and me to tell us about Dillon, I hadn't answered those calls. I had thrown away the letters. Deleted the emails.

I had done everything I could to ignore the fact that Cameron was my blood because I was just so pissed.

I was hurt, and I had lashed out. And I had been a fucking idiot.

So, I hadn't known that Dillon was my brother until he showed up at Cameron's side, an eighteen-year-old kid about to start college and in need of a family.

Cameron had helped to raise the kid, and I hadn't been there.

I had lost my brother, more than one actually, and I would never forgive myself.

But now the kid was here, and we were doing okay. Cameron and I had talked things out, and Brendon and I had done the same since Brendon had taken my cue and cut out Cameron, as well.

It had been a few months now, but I was getting used to the fact that Dillon was my brother. It was even kind of cool.

He wasn't too much of an idiot, even though he had done some pretty stupid things when he was a younger teenager. Like lying about applying for colleges. Because of that, he missed out on his first semester. Cameron had torn him a new one, but I thought Dillon had learned his lesson. Now, the kid was finally in the middle of his first semester at UCD, taking some gen-ed courses while he figured out what he wanted to do.

Although I had a feeling he was going to end up in culinary school like me. That was pretty cool. The fact that the kid I hadn't really known, the one that I hadn't helped raise, wanted to follow in my footsteps...yeah, pretty cool.

I didn't think it had anything to do with me, though. Because, like I said, even though my ego was pretty large, I wasn't that much of an idiot. Okay, I was, but still.

Dillon just liked working with food, enjoyed figuring out new recipes and trying some of the basics. And he was really damn good at it.

So, I didn't mind taking the extra time and steps to teach Dillon what I knew to get him prepared if he *did* want to go to culinary school.

We would see what would happen with that, though I liked the idea of Dillon taking that route. But I wouldn't push him. He'd been pushed enough by our birth mom, and I wouldn't be that asshole. Not again.

"You're staring at me," Dillon said, tilting his head as he studied my face. "What's wrong? Do you need some water or something?"

I shook my head and then rubbed my temple. "I'm fine."

"You have a headache?" Dillon popped up from the couch. "I can go get you a pain pill."

"I'm fine. Really. I have a headache because I didn't

sleep well. But I already took the one pain pill I'm allowing myself for the day. My hand doesn't hurt that much anymore, which is nice."

"You're taking the prescribed dose though, right?" Cameron asked, stuffing his hands into his pockets. "Don't make yourself hurt because you're afraid of what our mother did. Okay?"

We were all doing really good about just putting those fears and words out in the open. We used to hide the fact that we were afraid we would end up drug addicts and alcoholics like our birth parents, but we were getting better at the whole communication thing.

Probably because of the women in our lives.

No, the women in my brothers' lives.

Cameron had Violet. Brendon had Harmony. And I had...well, I didn't have anyone. And that was fine with me.

But Sienna was around. Or, at least, she had been. And so was Meadow, their new friend that was hanging out with them. I rubbed my hand over my heart, trying not to think about who *wasn't* with us.

Allison. My old friend. My ex-girlfriend. The one that wasn't around anymore.

But I wasn't going to think about that. Not when I was already hurting and surrounded by my brothers who wanted to make sure I was okay. Thinking about the fact that Allison was dead would not help my mood.

"If you're okay, then I won't go get you another pain pill. Promise," Dillon said quickly, filling the awkward silence.

"I am fine. And I'm taking the prescribed dose. But I'm not going to take any soon because I don't really need it. I know our family comes from a line of addicts, I'm not going to become one of those."

"I know you won't. But it also means that you may end up more in pain than you need to be and heal slower because you're afraid of becoming that."

"I'd flip you off, but my favorite middle finger is currently bandaged right now."

Brendon grinned at that and shook his head before taking a seat on the recliner next to my couch.

"You're a laugh riot, brother."

"I try." I paused. "So, have you heard anything about Sienna? Is she doing okay?" I tried to make my voice sound casual, probably too casual, and I likely wasn't fooling anyone in the room. Even the kid knew it was weird.

"We haven't really heard too much about her."

"I talked to Violet earlier, and she said Sienna's fine. Her bruises are healing up, and everything is doing good.

She's even working. You haven't talked to her?" Cameron asked, his voice deceptively calm.

"Not really. I don't really talk to Sienna every day. Unless I see her at the bar." Not quite true, but we tended to fight with each other more than anything. We just had personalities that clashed sometimes, and that meant we yelled at each other when we needed to get things done. It had even been like that when we were younger in school surrounded by all our friends, we had always been the ones to yell at each other.

That was just life.

Sienna was my short stack, the dork that I enjoyed hanging out with, even if she got under my skin sometimes.

And the fact that I kept thinking about her with those bruises on her body made me want to fight and hurt someone.

"The girls said that she's doing fine. We should see her at the bar tomorrow or so. She's just busy, trying to deal with the cops and figuring out who could have done it. But I don't know if they're going to actually figure that out." Brendon shrugged, but I could see the tension in his shoulders.

It seemed that none of us were actually truly okay with what had happened. Sienna had been hurt, could have died, could have had something even more horrible happen to her, and I hadn't been there for her.

It was all my fault.

And people saying that it wasn't, wasn't going to make me feel any better. So, I didn't say anything.

Because I didn't like the idea of Sienna hurt. Didn't like the idea of any of my friends getting hurt.

But, Sienna? The one person I got to talk to about stupid shit?

For some reason, the thought of her getting hurt made my gut clench, made my one non-injured hand that I had left fist at my side.

"Have you even called her?" Dillon asked.

"I texted her," I said shortly. "She didn't text back. I figured she was busy. Or didn't want to talk to me."

My brothers gave each other looks, and I ignored them. I really didn't want to get into this. I just wanted to make sure that she was okay, but that didn't mean I needed to learn anything else.

"Well, we should be able to see her tomorrow. And that means you can go back to the kitchen tomorrow, right?" Dillon said quickly. "Because I'm going to be right by your side. I'll be your hands. I mean, not as good as you, but I think I'm doing pretty well with a knife."

That made me smile. Even with all the shit going on, that did make me smile.

"Yeah, you're pretty damn good. But you need a lot more training. So, yeah, you'll be my hands. But getting back in that kitchen? That's something I really need to fucking do."

"Then you will."

We started talking about the business and the fact that the guys were going right back there a little bit later. Beckham was working on the opening, but we still had more to do. And all the while we were talking, I couldn't help but think about Sienna.

Just because her bruises were healing didn't mean everything else was. Because I didn't know if she was really fine.

Sometimes things were beneath the surface.

And I really didn't know if anyone knew Sienna.

Let alone me.

CHAPTER THREE

I'm the queen of awkward. Awkwardly.

-Sienna, age 15.

SIENNA

"WHY AM I HERE?" I asked the table and then shook my head, wondering why I was such a mess. "Sorry, I actually like being here, I'm just out of sorts."

I looked over at Violet, who leaned across the table and gave me a quick hug. "You're here because you're my sister and I love you, and we're going to have a drink if you want. Regardless, we are going to eat some amazing food. Aiden is back there, and though he's not using his hands, he is directing and yelling and doing his most Aiden of Aiden things. Dillon is back there helping him, as well. And I think the two are getting along. But that means we're going to get some amazing food, and you are going to breathe and just enjoy yourself for tonight. I know you've been at home or at work for the past week, but it's time for you to just hang out with us. Okay?"

I looked at Violet and nodded, but I wasn't really sure I believed her. Or if I believed myself.

"I'm such a dork right now. I'm sorry. I mean, I love this place. I loved it when it was Jack and Rose's, and I love it even more now that the Connolly brothers are running it. And you sort of have an in with one of the owners, and Harmony over here has another in."

"I'll be sure to let Brendon know that I think of him as my *in*," Harmony said, sipping her drink.

"I feel like I'm a little left out that I don't have an in here," Meadow said, playing with the condensation on her water glass. "Of course, I know you guys, and you guys have an in with the owners, so do I have an in with the in?"

I shook my head, laughing with Meadow. I really liked her, even though she didn't speak often. She was just sweet and always there for my sister, and it was nice to see her out and about.

She was usually at home alone, working hard, but she was out to hang out with me. Actually, here to hang out with all of us.

And I was glad because I didn't really want to be alone.

I rolled my neck and winced. My sister didn't miss the movement.

"What's wrong? Are you okay? Is it the bruising?" She said the latter very softly, and I was grateful. Although I might be loud and usually relished being the center of attention, I didn't like it when it had to do with my health or the fact that I could still remember the feeling of that man's fingers on my skin.

I didn't want to remember any of that.

"I'm fine. Really. I didn't take a pain pill today because I don't need them anymore, and I only have a twinge when I actually move wrong. So, I can have a nice beer and just enjoy myself."

Violet studied my face and gave me a tight nod. "Well, if that changes, you need to let me know. And the beer you have in front of you is one of the new ales that Cameron found. They're just putting it in bottles right now, but apparently, the brewery is going to draft soon, which is like a big thing. I think." Her nose scrunched, and I laughed. "I really don't know much about beer. Or wine. Other than what I like. Dating someone who owns a bar is actually quite enlightening."

"Tell me about it," Harmony said, and the two clinked their drinks.

I met Meadow's gaze, and we both laughed.

"I feel like I should probably date into the bar, what do you think? I mean, I feel like I need more than just an in of an in."

I didn't fail to notice that Meadow's gaze went to the bearded bartender for just a moment before she quickly moved back to looking directly at me.

I knew that Beckham looked at Meadow, as well, but the two didn't really seem to talk. Nor did they really hang out together other than at a few pool tournaments when I hadn't been around.

I swallowed hard, trying not to think about the reason I hadn't been at that last pool tournament.

Because I wasn't going to think about that.

I wasn't going to think about the awkwardness. About the fact that Aiden and I still hadn't talked about it.

About the fact that I didn't *want* to talk about it.

"You're off in your head again. What's wrong?" Violet asked. "You're not drinking your beer either."

I smiled widely, shaking off those thoughts, and took a

big gulp. It was nice, not too hoppy, and a little bit sweet. The perfect beer for me.

"It tastes amazing. Sorry, you know me, just blah blah blah in my head."

"You usually blah blah blah outside your head. You never shut up." Violet winked as she said it, and I rolled my eyes.

"Be nice."

"I am nice. I'm the nice one."

"No, Mace is the nice one. You're the weird one. And I'm the annoying one."

"Did you just call our big brother the nice one?"

"Maybe. He *is* the nice one. Well, Adrienne makes him the nice one."

"You're talking about your brother? The big, bearded tattoo artist?" Harmony asked. "Well, he actually *is* kind of nice. The few times that I've met him anyway."

"He is sweet. So sweet. I mean, have you seen him with his daughter?" Violet clutched her chest over her heart and rolled her eyes. "I mean, who would have thought the big Grumpy Gus would fall in love and help raise a beautiful little girl."

"When is their wedding again?" I asked, trying to remember if Adrienne and Mace had set a date.

"Not set yet. Apparently, all of the Montgomery

women are getting married or remarried, and so they're all planning different weddings."

Our brother Mace was marrying Adrienne Montgomery, who was part of a large family. Everyone had slowly started to fall in love and get engaged over the past couple of years, much like my friends up here.

Harmony and Violet were practically engaged to their men, yet here I was, alone, trying not to think about the last time I'd had sex.

Because I was not going to think about that.

Or him.

I reached out to grab my beer and twisted my wrist right at the wrong moment. "Fuck," I muttered.

Violet was right there, helping me with my glass. "Are you sure you're not in too much pain?"

I rubbed my wrist softly. "I'm fine. The bruises are healing. I promise."

"You say that, but I'm afraid. Just talk to me. Okay?"

"I am talking to you. They're going to find the men who came at me. I know it. I trust the police."

"I trust them, too," Harmony said. "But there's not a lot of evidence to help find those guys. And it was so close to here." Harmony shivered, and I reached out to rub her arm.

"It's going to be fine." I *was* going to be okay.

"You're not supposed to be the one trying to help me,"

Harmony said quickly. "I'm supposed to be the one helping you."

"You know what can help me? Forgetting it all happened. Because if we can just forget it all happened, it'll be okay."

As soon as I said that, Cameron came out, holding a tray of appetizers and tapas for us. I looked at the food and then remembered that I couldn't actually forget that it had happened.

Because I wasn't the only one who had gotten hurt.

"Hey, ladies, I have what you ordered here. And Aiden and Dillon added a few extra things. We have those chicken nachos that I know you love. And Dillon made these since I was really happy for them. There are some wings, but they're the Korean-fried wings rather than the buffalo ones. There's also a dip that I think has crab in it, but I'm not a hundred percent sure because he was mumbling it quickly, and it's not on the menu yet. There are also two types of side salads that are more communal than just for yourself. If none of this is to your liking, I'm sure I can bully my brother into making something else."

My mouth watered looking at everything that he was putting on the table, and I shook my head. "Don't bother him, I'm sure everything's going to be great."

Cameron gave me a look, his brows raised. "Wow, are

you sure you're okay? I've never actually seen you defend Aiden like that."

I froze, blinking. "I'm not mean to him." Everyone gave me a look. "Am I?"

Harmony cleared her throat. "You're not the sweetest to him. But he's not the sweetest to you either. You both are very..."

"Caustic towards one another," Violet said. "But not mean. Just...you guys like to rile each other up."

"Well, he has a broken hand. He shouldn't even be in the kitchen right now."

"We kept him out as long as we could," Cameron said softly. "But he knows what he's doing. He's not overdoing it."

I met Cameron's gaze and nodded, hoping he didn't actually see what was behind my thoughts.

Aiden had been hurt because of me. He wasn't doing what he loved right now, what he was amazing at, all because of me. And I didn't really know what to do about that.

"Okay," Violet said, clapping her hands. "We're going to eat all of this food. I don't care that Cameron's probably going to have to roll me home."

Cameron leaned down and pressed a hard kiss to her lips. "Don't worry about it, babe. Eat all you want. I'll carry you out of here."

"Even if it takes a forklift?" Violet asked.

"Even then."

She elbowed him in the gut, and he just laughed before kissing her again and walking away.

The place was busy tonight, and I was grateful for it. That meant that Cameron and Brendon were off doing their own things and not at our table. And that also meant they weren't going to be too overprotective with me and bothering me.

I loved the guys. I loved the fact that they were back in my life, but every time I looked at them, I was reminded that Aiden had been hurt. That he wasn't here. Yes, it was his first time back in the kitchen since the attack, but it still hurt to think about.

Everything hurt to think about.

"This is amazing," Meadow said, moaning. "Like how does he make this sauce?" she said after biting into one of the wings.

I took one from the plate and blew on it since it was still hot. As I took a bite, I held back a moan of my own. It was a perfect mix of crunch and sweetness and spiciness. I didn't know how he did it, but I was in love.

Not with Aiden.

But with his food.

I couldn't be in love with Aiden. Just because I had

been when I was younger, didn't mean I was *still* in love with him.

Aiden had fallen for Allison back when we were in school, and I had been the perpetual third wheel. Yes, I'd had other dates and boyfriends along the way, but I had always been invited into their relationship. Not in a sexual way or even an emotional way, but more in the idea that they never pushed me away if I ended up spending too much time with them. I loved Allison, loved her with everything I had. She was my best friend. Yes, Violet was my sister and a good friend to me, and Harmony was another best friend, but Allison was special.

Out of the four of us, I had always spent the most time with Allison. We were the two closest in age, and we just clicked.

Back in the day, Aiden and I had clicked as well, but he had fallen in love with my best friend.

So, I had watched the two of them get all lovey-dovey and lose their virginities to each other. Well, not actually *watched* them, but I had been there for the aftermath when they'd both been all awkward and then not so awkward.

I held back a smile at that memory, eating more of my wing. They had been amazing to each other, and then they hadn't. They'd drifted apart yet remained friends and still kept me in their friendship circle. But I'd always had a thing for Aiden, even when I shouldn't have.

And when everybody went their separate ways—at least the guys—I'd still had a slight crush on him, even though he hadn't been in my life.

Now, he was back, and Allison was gone. Just the idea that I could still have a crush on him made my stomach revolt slightly.

Because it didn't matter that it had been almost a decade since Allison and Aiden were together. He had been hers.

He wasn't mine. He couldn't be mine.

And now, every time I looked at him, I would think about the fact that he had been hurt because of me, and it complicated things. Because I hadn't been strong enough to protect myself, and he had been forced to come to the rescue.

"Are you going to just stare at that bone?" Violet asked. "Do you want to go home, Sienna? We can just go home and forget all about this."

"I'm fine. I promise." I set down my chicken wing bone and picked up my appetizer plate so I could pile it with nachos. "I'm starving. And the food's amazing."

"Dillon did great," Harmony agreed. "Brendon said that he's really taken to cooking and all the other aspects of it. And Aiden's been helping. Even when he's growling about his hand."

I held back a wince, but I was pretty sure Violet saw it anyway. My sister was far too good at reading my moods, and I hated that sometimes.

Meadow moaned. "I think I'm in love with this salad, is there crab in it?"

"Yes, it's like a fish salad but not as gross as it sounds."

"How does a fish salad sound gross?" I asked, piling another plate with both of the salads. I was apparently starving. And Aiden was an amazing cook. Even if he was just showing Dillon how to make it happen.

"I don't know, it just sounds weird to me. But Aiden knows what he's doing."

"Yes, he does," Brendon said, winking at us as he came forward with another tray.

"This time, he's made you a cheese plate. So, he didn't actually do any cooking with this, but there are some jams and honeys that he got from locally-sourced areas, and all the cheese is locally-sourced, as well." He set it down in front of us, and I swore I drooled.

"I'm going to gain so much weight, but I don't care. Oh my God, is that brie?"

"Try it with the honey on this bread that Aiden baked earlier."

I looked up. "He baked the bread?"

"He did everything except for the kneading. Dillon did that while Aiden just glowered over him."

"Aiden does glower a lot," Meadow said quickly. "But I think that's just his resting face."

That made Brendon throw his head back and laugh. "Oh my God, I have to tell him that. Instead of resting bitch face, he has a resting glower face."

"RGF?" Harmony asked. "I kind of like that. Of course, I think all of you Connollys sometimes get it. He just happens to have the worst of it." Brendon leaned forward and kissed Harmony softly, a gentle, lingering kiss that sent shivers down my spine. "He just needs a woman."

Brendon gave me a look before he stood back up again, and I pointedly ignored him.

I knew the others thought that there had to be something between us considering how much we fought, but there wasn't.

And there wasn't going to be.

Despite that night.

No, I wasn't going to think about that.

"I didn't think I was starving before this, but I'm going to help finish everything on this table. I hope that's okay," I said to Brendon, shaking my head. "Because this looks amazing."

"It *is* amazing. I taste-tested everything while he was

making it in the back." He patted his belly. "I'm having to work out twice as hard just to get over the fact that my little brother is an amazing chef and trying out new recipes here."

Harmony narrowed her eyes and licked her lips. "Oh, I'm sure we can find ways for you to work out."

I snorted, quickly filling my mouth with food so I wouldn't say something inappropriate. Harmony was usually a little prim, a bit proper. But ever since she and Brendon had declared their love for each other, some of my own antics were coming out of her. Or maybe it was just her inner thoughts. Brendon was a bit more upper-crust than the rest of his brothers, even though he had come from the same streets that they had. He just tended to be a little more business-like. Brendon and my friend worked well together, but from the looks exchanged between them, I was afraid I was going to get pregnant just watching the two of them. Sheesh.

Brendon left us alone, and Meadow left the table for a moment to go up to the bar and talk to the female bartender that the brothers had hired.

Not Beckham.

Interesting. I didn't know what was said, but it looked like the two women knew each other before Meadow came back to the table, smiling. "Sorry, I know her son. I tutored him a few times. I was just wondering how she was doing."

I looked up at Jersey and nodded. "Oh, yeah, I forgot she has a teenage son. You tutor?" I asked.

"Not often. But that was a special case. Anyway, I really don't think I can eat another bite."

"I don't think I can either," I said. I pushed my plate away, even though it was completely clean. "Okay, I think I ate half of what was on this table."

"Well, you haven't really been eating for the past week. I'm glad that you stuffed your face."

I looked up. "Well, Violet, I'm not going to pass up wings, nachos, and the best salads ever," I said, laughing.

"Hell no, you're not," Violet said, leaning back as she patted her stomach.

I stood up from the table and stretched, ignoring the way my skin hurt. My whole body still hurt, and I was grateful that it hadn't been worse, but it still wasn't the best.

"I'm going to use the restroom, I'll be right back."

Violet stood up too, and I shook my head. "I can go by myself. I'm safe here."

"You can go by yourself, yes, but I thought girls traveled in packs to the bathroom."

"Just let me go by myself. I promise I'll be good. I'll be quick."

Violet gave me a long look but then nodded before sitting back down.

It didn't matter that I figured that Violet actually did have to use the restroom, I just wanted to do one thing on my own and prove that I could. I was probably being an idiot, but I couldn't help it. Inside, I was shaking, trying to get back to my old self. It wasn't going to be easy.

I turned the corner down the hall and smacked right into a very hard chest.

A hard chest that I knew. Intimately.

My hands went to Aiden's pecs, and I looked up, blinking.

"Are you okay?" he asked, his voice soft.

"I'm fine. Sorry for bumping into you."

"I'm sorry, too." He took a step back, and I missed the warmth, but I told myself that was fine. "The guys told me you were here."

"The food was amazing." I looked down at his bandaged hand and swallowed hard. My eyes burned, but I ignored it. I would not cry. I would not.

"You and Dillon did a great job."

He looked down at his hand and snorted. "Dillon did a great job. I just ordered him around."

"I guess you're good at that." I winced, annoyed at myself for saying it like that. But Aiden just smiled. The action brightened his face. I'd missed that smile. But I told myself it was fine. I didn't deserve that expression. Because he had been hurt because of me.

"We should talk. Soon. We need to."

I met his gaze and shook my head. "No. We can't. We don't need to."

I turned away. I couldn't stand to look at him. Not because he had done anything wrong. But because every time I saw him, I remembered what had happened in that alley, and I remembered that it was my fault that he was hurt. I just needed some time apart.

We had already needed time apart before the attack, and this just solidified it.

He reached for me, but I quickly took a step back.

When he cursed under his breath, I just sighed.

"I'm not going to hurt you."

"I know you won't. But I need to go."

"Sienna."

"I need to go," I repeated. I practically ran towards the table and picked up my purse. The others looked at me, worry clear in their gazes.

"I need to go, I'm not feeling well."

"I'll go with you," Violet said. "You shouldn't go out alone."

"I need to."

"I'm walking that way anyway," Meadow said softly. "My car's parked right next to yours. We'll just go. We don't even have to talk. But don't walk alone tonight, at least for everyone else's peace of mind."

I looked at my friends and nodded.

"Fine."

I said my goodbyes and tried to act like everything was casual. But it wasn't.

Nothing was casual about this.

I had parked closer to the bar tonight, and for that I was grateful. Everything was lit up, everything was safe, and I was very much aware that Aiden and Cameron were outside, watching us walk to our cars.

I was never alone these days, and I didn't think I was going to be truly alone like I had been that night again.

My friends wouldn't let me.

I said goodbye to Meadow, waved at the guys near the bar, and got into my car, driving home even as I shook.

I didn't know what was wrong with me.

Yeah, I was trying to deal with the attack, but it was more that every time I saw Aiden, everything just came back to the surface, and I didn't know how to deal with it.

I was just exhausted and full. And I really needed to pee.

This was my life now, one never-ending weirdness after another.

I pulled into my driveway, got out, and checked my

mail. There was no one around. It was a relatively quiet street, and I was grateful.

I pulled out my bills and whatever junk mail they had given me, and then pulled out a single red rose.

I froze, wondering why that would be in my mailbox. Maybe it had been one of my neighbors. The couple next door, Jeff and Dave, were wonderful and had been so supportive after the attack. They, along with my sister, had baked and cooked for me so I wouldn't even have to make dinner. It had probably been them, wanting to make sure that I was taken care of and knew I was loved.

But I still looked at the rose, wondering how and why it could be there.

For an instant, I thought maybe it could be from Aiden, but that would never be.

He wasn't the roses type.

And, anyway, it didn't matter. Because he wasn't mine.

Nothing was mine.

Never again.

CHAPTER FOUR

AIDEN

I HADN'T BEEN HERE in over a month. I probably should have come before this, but it wasn't the easiest thing for me. Hell, it *shouldn't* be easy, and I guess that's why I was here at all.

I lowered myself to the ground and set the single tulip on Allison's grave.

"Sorry it took me so long to get here. Wasn't sure what to say. What I *needed* to say. Or even if you wanted me here." I shrugged, knowing no one was around to listen to me, and hell, I didn't even know if Allison could hear me.

Throughout my life, I'd thought a lot about death, mostly because it was something that I figured a lot of people did. At first, it had been because I was afraid I was going to die when I was a kid. Not because of some illness or sickness I couldn't control, but because my mother was just that bad of a parent. I didn't even know who my father was, only that I shared him with Cameron. I didn't share my father with Dillon. No one knew who Dillon's father was.

And then when I had gone into the foster system, for some reason, I had always thought death was lurking, just waiting to take me away. Maybe that was easier than trying to figure out how to grow up without a family or even a pillow to call your own.

I hadn't thought about death as much when I moved in with Jack and Rose. When they took me in and called me a Connolly. When they did the same with my twin and then with Brendon.

It was easier to grow up thinking that maybe you were invincible when you actually had someone to rely on. When you figured out that perhaps someone would be there to kiss your wounds or take you to the hospital if you actually hurt yourself worse than just a scrape from a fall off your bike.

So, I hadn't thought about death as much until I got older when I learned how to drive.

I thought about going too fast on curves, or what would happen if I accidentally went off a bridge.

Little things that were actually more commonplace than most people thought.

Just little instances in your life where you thought about death, and then you forgot about it because you were alive. You weren't sick. You were whole.

I hadn't really thought about death when I was in college, other than just trying not to make the mistake of accidentally hurting myself by drinking too much or driving too fast.

I had thought about death right at the end of my relationship with Allison, though.

Not because either of us was sick or because I'd thought I wanted to die.

Because we had held death between us.

And then I had moved on. I became an adult and learned how to be a real grownup that actually had to deal with a job and health insurance and a 401K.

I'd only thought about death in the abstract because it was something that came for all of us. I just figured it'd be when I was older. Because I had been lucky that I wasn't sick. Lucky that I'd lived through all the things that could've taken someone out quickly.

I hadn't thought about death again until I'd gotten the call that the first person I ever loved wasn't here anymore.

"I hate the fact that I'm angry, Allison." I swallowed hard and traced my finger across her name in the cold stone. I expected it to cut like a blade, not to feel smooth under my skin. "I'm always angry these days. And I hate the fact that I'm angry with you. You weren't supposed to die, Allison. You were supposed to outlive all of us because you smiled. Because you were so damn happy about everything. But it'd been a while since I'd seen you, right? Maybe I was only thinking about the girl you had been. The girl I loved."

I didn't cry, but I did pinch the bridge of my nose, forcing the emotion back. I was too angry to think about anything else. Too upset to feel sad, to feel the over-whelming urge to just weep about the fact that Allison was gone.

No, I was too angry for that.

"I don't know why you had to do that. I wish I knew the answer. I wish I knew why or would've seen it. I wish I would've actually been in your life more than I was. But I wasn't there. And I'm not asshole enough to think I would've been able to stop it. I don't know why you did it, Allison. And I hate myself more every day for the fact that I wasn't there."

I shook my head and let my eyes close, the sun warm on my face.

"That makes me a selfish asshole, doesn't it? Because what you did had nothing to do with me. We had nothing to do with each other for long enough that I don't even know why you did it. But your friends don't either, Allison. I look at Violet, Sienna, and Harmony. I look at them, and I see the same confusion that I have. And I hate the fact that we don't have answers. And that we might not ever. But maybe that's on us. Maybe we should've been able to see." I let out a shaky breath and opened my eyes, trailing my fingers across her name again.

"I hope you're with her." I whispered the words, this time my throat closing as I forced myself not to cry. "I hope to God that isn't why you're here. But...I just hope you're with her. I loved you, Allison. I still do. And I hate the fact that you're gone. And sometimes...sometimes, I just hate the fact that I'm here."

I wiped away the fallen leaves and stray pieces of grass that dared to venture onto the new mound of soil that was Allison's grave and just tried to soak in the sun. I tried not to feel the overwhelming sense that I was doing something wrong.

My hand hurt, even though it was healing, and everything else hurt just because I wasn't sleeping enough and wasn't doing anything that was normally on my schedule.

I really hated the fact that Allison was here. I remembered once when we were talking about what we wanted if one of us died, long before we had thought it'd be an issue. But we each talked about cremation and having our ashes thrown to the wind. Maybe in a place that we both loved, or somewhere that one of us wanted to visit. Just somewhere. But she hadn't made a will—none of us had. And her parents had done what they thought was best.

That meant no organ donation and no cremation. She'd been buried in a dress to match her eyes. Eyes that would never be open again. And now, she was here, taking up space.

Her words, not mine. Because I never thought Allison could take up space. Not in any way. But what did I know? I was just the guy who had once loved her. The guy who still loved her, only not in the same way that I had when we were in love.

So, I sat there for a little bit longer and then I made my way back to my car, saying goodbye one more time.

I didn't know if I would be back. Didn't know if it would help anything. I was just feeling out of sorts lately, not able to do what I normally did. I couldn't work out the way I wanted, couldn't cook the way I wanted. Couldn't do anything the way I wanted. So, I had been feeling a little petulant and, because of that, I needed to center myself.

Though seeing the place where Allison had been laid to rest hadn't really helped like I thought it would.

Nothing helped these days.

I got home, anger still coursing in my veins just

because I felt useless. But I would go to work later, and maybe things would fall into place.

I liked living in Denver, well at least in the suburbs. I wasn't really a downtown guy, though I worked there. I had worked there before I started at the bar, although it had been at a Michelin-starred restaurant where I never would've moved up because of the nepotism.

It hadn't mattered that I was a better chef than any of the people in there. Hadn't mattered that I could run the place better than anyone I worked with. I hadn't been blood, so I hadn't been wanted.

And when Jack and Rose died, leaving the bar to us, I left.

Yeah, it was a step down to anyone who didn't know me, but I felt more like I was home at the brewery. I wasn't putting on airs, wasn't pretending that I was someone I wasn't. I was doing something for family. Something I hadn't done enough in recent times.

I just hated the fact that I couldn't actually do it now because I had broken my damn hand trying to protect Sienna.

And I hadn't even really seen her since the attack. Because she didn't want to talk to me. She had fucking *run* from me.

Just like she had run from me after the one night we'd had.

But I wasn't going to think about that.

I really wanted a beer, but it was in the middle of the afternoon, and I still had to work later. So, I opened myself a soda, something I didn't really want, but I needed a boost of caffeine. My front door opened as soon as I took the first sip, and I glared at Cameron as he walked in.

"What did I say about using that key for emergencies?"

"You probably wouldn't have let me in if I'd knocked." Cameron just shrugged as he closed the door behind him, and I glared.

"Well, you didn't give me the option, did you? I could've been walking around naked in here."

"We're twins. Pretty sure I know what you have."

"We may be identical, but maybe not in every single way," I snapped.

"Okay, do you want to compare dicks? Because I can whip mine out right now and show you exactly what I have."

"Well, that's just weird," I said and snorted. "Like, really weird."

"You're the one that brought it up."

"Did I?"

"Oh, shut up. I'm here to check on you."

I flipped my twin off and took another sip. "I'm fine. Just like I was fine before. And I'm going to be fine later. I don't really need you all up in my business, acting like an asshole."

"Only one of us is acting like an asshole right now, and it's not me."

"Oh, fuck off."

"Sorry. Can't do that. Remember? You're my brother. And that means I get to annoy the shit out of you."

"Go annoy Brendon. Oh, wait, go annoy Dillon. He's the one who needs to be annoyed the most in our group."

"Yeah, I don't think so. Hey, did I tell you that we're thinking of putting him in the dorms or something close to that next year?" Cameron asked, and I stood up straighter.

"Dorm? Are you sure you want him to do that? I mean, is that the best place for a kid trying to find his feet?"

"I don't really know, but that whole band phase was just because he liked to hang out with his friends. Yeah, he fucked up, but he's better now. And he has us. Maybe he needs to hang out with kids his own age rather than almost-thirty-somethings that are old and haggard and broken." Cameron gestured to my hand, and then I used my free one once I set down my soda to flip him off again.

"That's going to be expensive. You okay with that?"

"It's fine. I don't really want him to get student loans since our economy's in the tank and you can never pay those things off these days."

"Dear God. When did we get old?"

"I have no idea, and I don't know if I like it. But Violet likes me, so I'm going to call it a win."

"Hell, you're whipped."

"Very much so, and I like it. Maybe you should get whipped."

"I'm not into that kinky shit. I thought that was more Brendon's style."

"I'm really not going to touch that subject," Cameron said, holding up his hands in surrender. "Like really do not want to talk about that subject."

"Fine with me."

"Anyway, you need to get yourself a woman. Maybe that would stop this attitude of yours."

"Shut the fuck up. Back to Dillon, though, you really want him to stay in a dorm?"

"Maybe not a dorm. Maybe he needs to find some friends and live with them. He's welcome to stay with me for his entire college experience, but I feel like he's hiding within the walls of that bar. You know? Something that we all do very well."

"I'm not hiding."

"I said *we*. Not just you. But good to know you're on the right track of thinking about the fact that you are indeed hiding. As for Dillon? I don't know. I just want him to know that he has options. That he actually needs to socialize with human beings while he's in school. But not socialize too much that he fucks up his grades. There has to be a happy medium."

"He'll find it. He's a smart kid."

"I'm glad to hear you say that. I was really afraid when I came back here with him that you wouldn't want to talk to him at all. Or we'd fuck up our family even more."

I shook my head and took another sip of my drink. "I have to admit, I was really surprised when I first saw him. He looks so much like us, even though he's not our twin and only our half-brother. And I was angry at everything then. Angry at Mom. Angry at you. Angry at myself. And I sort of took it out on him by just ignoring him at first. But I think we're better now."

"You're a thousand percent better."

"You can't be more than a hundred percent."

"Whatever."

"Why are you here?" I asked, frowning. "I'm fine."

"Well..." Cameron began and then trailed off.

"Violet sent you here, didn't she?"

"You know it. Sienna ran out of the place so quickly last night, she was worried about her sister. Since you were in the hall last we saw, we figured maybe it had something to do with you. So, have anything to enlighten us with?"

"Not really. I don't know why she left." The anger

rose again, and I gritted my teeth, trying to tamp it down. No use breaking shit when it came to Sienna. Because there was no way I could try and figure out exactly what was going on between us. Because there wasn't anything going on between the two of us. "Violet's just worried about her."

My head shot up, and my eyes widened. "What's wrong? Is she okay?"

Cameron gave me a look, his brows raised. "You seemed a little overly curious."

"Shut up. Is she okay?"

"She's fine. At least physically. But she's not talking about what happened, and then she ran away from the bar. Yeah, we were all watching her, but it was a little out of the blue. We just want to make sure she's fine. And since you were the last one to really talk with her, it might be helpful if you told us what you talked about."

"So you're blaming this on me? You don't have to. I already do enough of it on my own. Maybe if I'd actually remembered my damn phone and hadn't left her, she wouldn't have been attacked at all. So, yeah, it's my fucking fault she's hurt. But I'm not the one who forced her to run out of the bar last night. So, don't put that on me."

Cameron held up his hands. "That's not what I'm saying at all. I'm not blaming you for any of that. Sienna doesn't blame you for the fact that she was attacked. We blame those stupid idiots that came at her. The ones that held her down."

"Don't fucking tell me what happened to her in the alleyway. I don't want to relive it again. Because I saw it. You weren't there."

I hadn't been either.

But I didn't say that.

"What the hell is the matter with you? Sienna is physically fine. Your hand is going to heal. But there's something wrong with her. She needs to talk about it, and she's not. I was just wondering if she actually talked about it with you. But if you're going to act like an asshole, maybe I won't talk to you at all."

"Fine. Just fucking leave. It's what you're good at."

"That's uncalled for. I thought we were over that. But if you're going to throw that in my face, I'll just go. And leave you to deal with whatever the fuck is going on in your head."

Anger rushed through me, and I fisted my hand at my side before reaching out to the first thing I could grab before I threw it at the wall." Glass shattered, and Cameron just looked at me, his eyes narrowed, his jaw tense.

I looked down and saw the photo of when Cameron,

Brendon, and I were teenagers, glass all over the floor around the broken frame.

"Fuck," I muttered under my breath.

"You need to work out whatever's going on in your head. Because you're going to hurt yourself. If you don't figure out how to deal with your anger, deal with whatever guilt you have going on, something's going to happen. And we already lost Allison. I'm not going to lose you, too. So, get your head out of your ass and talk to one of us. Figure it out. While you're there, help us with Sienna. Because she's hurting, and Violet is worried. And if Violet is worried, then I'm worried. But I'm worried about you, too, Aiden. You're my brother. So, you're going to have to fucking deal with me. No matter what."

Cameron walked away, leaving me with the broken glass, and the rest of my mess.

I was an asshole. I was a fucking guilty asshole who didn't know how to deal with anything. I was just so pissed off at the world.

Because Allison was dead. Sienna had gotten hurt. And I couldn't do what I needed to.

It was all my damn fault.

Everything was my fault.

And I hated it all.

CHAPTER FIVE

Now I have guilt!

    -Sienna, age 5, thanks to endless viewings of Toy Story.

SIENNA

IT WAS nice to get into the swing of things again, even if sometimes my job wasn't the easiest thing in the world.

"You have to keep up with your treatments, Rocko," I said, shaking my head. I folded my hands over my chest and tried my best to look stern. But it was really hard to look that way when a man who had to be at least over a foot taller than me rocked back on his heels and looked like a little kid rather than a forty-something-year-old former football player.

"I know, it's just...sometimes it's really hard. You know?"

"I do. But we have the plan in place. And you're doing great things now. You're able to sit in a chair longer than you used to. And even go walking. But your back needs help. And that's what I'm here for."

"I know, Miss Knight. It's just hard. You know?"

I nodded, knowing we were going in circles again. But Rocko kept going on, and then we went through our checklist before he left for the day.

I was a physical therapist and worked at a clinic that focused on sports injuries. Ninety percent of my clients were former athletes. Not that you could really be a former athlete once you'd put your entire body and mindset into becoming one. But ones who were no longer at the peak of their careers and no longer worked professionally came to me. Their sports teams and other agencies would pay for the bigger-name clinics. But when they no longer had those options or wanted something a little smaller, they came to my clinic.

Not that it was actually *my* clinic, I was just one of the six physical therapists. I didn't own the place, but it was in my dreams to one day own and run my own clinic, much like this one.

I loved this place, though. They worked wonders for people and really cared about an athlete's body rather than what that body could do for the sports.

Don't get me wrong, I loved sports. I watched them, went to games, I had even played some in college and high school. Hell, I still played softball and even touch football with friends every once in a while. But I hated what professional sports did to an athlete's body.

So, it was my job to try and get those battered, bruised, and broken bodies into some form of shape. Not physical shape, but in a way where someone could actually have a fulfilling life without constant pain, fatigue, or even death at times.

Rocko was one of my many football players who had just run his body to the ground. He had been an offensive lineman, so he was big, a little bulky, and not very quick on his feet, but he had loved the game and had always protected his quarterback. And, because of that, he hadn't actually protected his body or his own back. So now, it was my job to make sure that he could sit in an airplane and not want to cry from the pain. That he could take a casual walk with his wife and not want to throw up. Rocko's knees and back were shot. It had taken over three years of working with me to get to the point where he could sit in his car and drive to see me.

Penalties came from throwing your life and body into professional sports. Sure, they paid you well, but you ruined your body by the age of twenty-five or thirty. I didn't think it was worth it, but then again, I liked being able to move.

Just the few days I had been sore and bruised from the attack had been enough.

I pushed those thoughts out of my mind and got my room ready for my next patient.

Jefferson was also a former football player, a quarterback. He was tall, broad-shouldered, and had a wicked smile. He also had a traumatic brain injury thanks to his sport, and sometimes had problems remembering to come in or recalling the conversations we had.

It was my job to work on his knees and his shoulders, but he refused to get help for everything else.

It didn't matter that he wore a helmet, helmet-to-helmet contact was still too much.

So, his brain was messing with him. And while it was my job to help his body, other people helped his mind. At least, that was the goal—if he'd let them.

"It's good to see you, Miss Knight." I gave him a small smile and nodded. "It's good to see you too, Jefferson. Did you do what we talked about last time?"

"I made a note and everything. See?" He pulled out a note from his back pocket, and I smiled. His mother usually came with him to these appointments, and for that, I was grateful. Sometimes, Jefferson was normal, or at least as normal as someone in his position could be. Other times, he got angry. Even more times, he just reverted back to a sweeter, younger version of himself.

I knew he got headaches and had other issues that came from having so many concussions while he was playing professional football.

But there was only so much I could do. Today, we were going to work on his shoulders.

And I could just hope that he was happy, at least as much as he could be.

I pushed all those thoughts out of my mind and went to work. I worked in the same gym area with the other therapists, but during this hour, I was alone with Jefferson. I didn't mind because I knew others would be around, and his mother was in the hallway. But sometimes I had to push back the thoughts that I was alone, much smaller than any of the men that I worked with, and a woman. I never used to think so much about that, even though it was always a constant note in my head. More like I could get through it. But then the alley happened. And I thought about it a bit more now.

I shook my head and then went back to what we had

been working on.

Jefferson was in pain a lot of the time, so our goal was to decrease that and restore mobility. Eventually, we'd increase strength and flexibility. But mostly, we just wanted to make sure that he could function. We didn't need to optimize his performance like some sports medicine people did because he was no longer a professional athlete. But some of my job was to prevent injuries and educate my clients on what they could do to not re-injure themselves. Because no matter what you did, you couldn't take the athlete out of some of these people. A lot of them still did charity events or just played with friends. And it could all lead to more injuries if they weren't careful.

What was funny to me, was that a lot of these guys with shoulder injuries just went off to golf in charity tournaments, thinking it wouldn't be that bad, only to hurt their shoulder again and need a whole new plan.

Today, we were working on Jefferson's shoulders, but I knew that next time we'd work on balance. And that meant I got to do my favorite thing, dancing.

All of my guys rolled their eyes at me when I brought it up, but they were light on their toes when flexibility and balance were key.

"Your bruises are going away," Jefferson said, glaring down at me.

I knew he wasn't actually glaring *at* me, more at what

had happened to me, but I still didn't like seeing the glare.

"I'm fine. You know me, it takes forever for this pale skin of mine to stop showing bruises." I pulled down the sleeve of my shirt. The only place there was still a bruise was on my wrist. And even then, it was so faded that you couldn't really tell it was there. I just happened to heal slowly, despite my profession.

"Now, let's work on your shoulders. Grip the handles and then pull back. We're on bands today, so you're going to have a little more give than you would on a machine."

He nodded at me, pulling his gaze from my wrist as he went to work.

We did a few reps and then worked on a couple of other things before I went to work on his shoulder, making sure we were all cooled down and ready to go.

I was tired but still had two more patients before the end of the day.

I loved my job, even if sometimes my own body hated me for it.

It didn't matter that I wasn't technically an athlete, working on athletes' bodies was hard on my own.

My next patient was Chad, a former wrestler, and so sweet. He had hurt his shoulders and his back quite severely when another wrestler in his collegiate league broke the rules and did a few things that he wasn't supposed to do.

Chad had been in a wheelchair for almost a year as he healed.

Now, Chad was walking and doing most things that anybody could do, but he still had some pain—something that was going to be forever now. An injury like that led to chronic pain, but that's why Chad came in twice a week to make sure he didn't injure himself further. He was still in his mid-twenties and had a long life to lead.

I just hated the fact that someone else's mistake had hurt him.

I took my lunch after Chad had left, knowing I was late doing that. I still needed to feed my body and my soul.

My last client of the day was a man named Marcus, a former track and field all-star athlete that had torn his ACL and injured his hamstring while training for the Olympics.

Marcus wouldn't be running in the Olympics anytime soon—or ever—and I didn't know how to help him mentally with that. But other people at my clinic knew how to help me lead him towards the right therapist since we could help with the body here but only so much with the mind.

"It feels better," Marcus said. "I let it run. You know, really run."

I gave him a smile but shook my head. I had to be firm,

even though I needed to be nice at the same time. "We need to go slow, Marcus. I know you hate that."

"There's nothing slow about me, Miss Knight." He gave me a wink, and I just rolled my eyes.

"I'm sure, but healing takes time. And if you don't want to have to deal with this again and again, especially at the exact wrong moment, you're going to have to listen."

We had gone over what his prospects were, and the fact that even with all the rehab and training in the world, his leg would never be as strong as it had been. We were going to try, but I wasn't going to give him false hope. I also wouldn't take his dreams away from him. It was a fine line, and sometimes I wasn't the best at handling it.

By the time I'd finished with Marcus, I was tired and still had some paperwork to do. The others were going to need the pieces of equipment that I had been using, so I moved out of the gym area and into my office. I had a small window, but it wasn't the biggest room in the place. I didn't mind, I was rarely in it anyway. I went through my files, looked at what I was doing for the rest of the week, and tried to maintain the plans that I had for each of my clients. It wasn't easy, trying to overlap what they needed with what they wanted, but sometimes, I could make it happen.

Being the person who had to tell others that maybe their dreams were over wasn't the easiest thing in the world. I hated being that person, but I also had to be the voice of reason and reality for others. I could help some reach their dreams, but most of the time, I was the one telling them that they needed to hold back.

And as someone who hated holding back herself, it wasn't easy.

By the time the sun was setting, I was all packed and ready to go home. I nodded at my coworkers as I left and put my keys between my fingers as I walked to my car. I didn't use my little cat ear thing anymore. It hadn't helped me before, and I didn't think keys between my knuckles were going to help this time if anything happened. Maybe I needed to get pepper spray. Or at least learn to use it. Or perhaps I just needed to be stronger. Or at a minimum, not afraid to walk to my car when there was still sun, and I was parked right under a light.

I hated this fear, but I didn't think it was going away anytime soon.

The drive home took forever. Traffic and I never got along. By the time I got home, I just wanted to eat, bury myself in whatever leftovers I had in my fridge, and cuddle with my cats.

I grinned down at them as Baby ran towards me.

She'd had another name when I pulled her from the foster home, but she'd ended up being Baby. She pranced towards me, dancing around my feet, and I set my stuff down on the entryway table before picking her up.

"Did you have a fun day?" I asked, nuzzling the top of her head before petting her. She purred into me and started chirping.

I wasn't really a crazy cat lady if I talked to my cats and they answered back, right? I mean, cats could totally talk. They understood you.

Right?

I really hoped no one else would ever answer those questions for me. Because I really didn't want to know the answer.

I walked into the kitchen and shook my head. "So? Did we have a rave?" I put Baby down on the floor, and she purred near me before prancing off into a full gallop towards the living room.

"Well, at least some things don't change." I shook my head and started closing all the cabinet doors. Somehow, the cats had learned to open every single cabinet in the house. And when they got lonely or annoyed with me or each other, they would open the cabinet doors. The shelving units that I had inside the cabinets were those soft-closing ones, which meant that they couldn't actually get into them themselves. It was great for organizing, but the cats hated it. It also meant that they just left the cabinet doors open, and I had to close them. I used to have child locks on everything, but my hands had hated it, and it only really discouraged me from getting into the cabinets rather than the cats. So, I had taken them off, much to my brother's and sister's amusement.

I picked up two of the water bowls on my first floor and cleaned them out to fill them up again, right as Danger and Moxie made their way into the kitchen. Moxie was my second youngest, a really quiet boy who was a little skittish. Although he wasn't skittish when it came to the UPS man. Why, I didn't know. But Moxie loved the UPS guy. Moxie didn't like me too much, but I was gaining traction. It had only taken three years. Maybe in another three years, he would actually let me pick him up.

I took a couple of very soft steps towards Moxie and held out my hand. When Moxie sniffed it twice and didn't back away, I counted that as a win.

"It's good to see you too, boy," I said softly. Moxie ran, and I just shook my head. Well, that had been a win.

I went over to where Danger was drinking his water and petted him. Danger just looked at me, maybe winked, and then went back to his water. Danger was my lazy baby. So lazy in fact, I was very surprised that he was actually out walking around like this. I looked at the time and shook my head. Ah, it was wet food time.

Six thirty on the dot every night, the cats got wet food.

And that was the only reason Danger would be away from his very comfortable bed. There could be an actual tornado in front of my house, and Danger probably wouldn't get out of bed. He was that lazy.

I quickly got four of their little plates and set their food on each one evenly, then added some water and set three of them down on the floor. Danger, Moxie, and Baby ran towards the food and started eating. I looked down at the fourth plate and shook my head. "This is getting ridiculous," I whispered to myself. But I was the cat lady, trademark and everything, and that meant I had to do what my cats said. So, I took the fourth plate, pulled a beer from the fridge, somehow twisted off the cap with just one hand, and made my way upstairs.

Runway, my eldest baby who was now ten years old, smiled up at me from the bedroom. She was nestled in a pile of pillows on my bed, and I just shook my head at her. She didn't like the other babies, *really* didn't like them, so therefore, she rarely came downstairs. Oh, she came some-times, and I was very careful not to move too quickly and scare any of the other cats and therefore scare her when she did. But Runway was sweet. She just liked people, not cats.

"Okay, come with me to the bathroom so you can have your food." Somehow, I had done the one thing I said I would never do. I had a special place where Runway could eat and just be. It encroached on my space, and I really didn't have any place to call my own in my house anymore. Because I didn't live alone. I lived with four cats who owned the place. I just rented from them.

I petted Runway softly, rubbing her soft fur, and then used the brush on her since the other cats wouldn't bathe her. Or rather, she wouldn't *let* them bathe her.

"I think I have a problem," I said to her. She looked up at me and burped before going back to her food.

She didn't usually eat this calmly, but she knew I was there to protect her in case any other cat came up from behind. Not that they would, but she was as paranoid as I was these days.

My sister and brother were happy in their relationships and talking about future children and everything. Harmony was on her second serious relationship and totally in love with Brendon, and I knew they were going to get married soon.

And I was just fine being alone.

Because I had my cats.

"Dear God."

I took a sip of my beer, sat on the toilet lid, and watched my cat eat her food so she wouldn't be alone. And when she was finished, I drained the last of my beer and brought the plate down so I could wash it with the rest of the other cats' empty dishes.

I heated up my leftovers in the microwave and ate in the kitchen so I didn't make a mess anywhere else.

I really wasn't this pathetic usually. It just seemed like it to me right then.

My phone was by my hand as I finished up the dishes, and I looked down at it, knowing I needed to take the next step.

Aiden had been hurt because of me. And I needed to do better and check on him. I hated the fact that I had run away like I did, worried because he had said we needed to talk. I needed to do better in a lot of things. So, the first thing I would do was text him.

Me: *Hey.*

Oh, that was good. Hey. That was like the greatest way to start a conversation.

Aiden: *Hey. Just about to work in the kitchen. You okay?*

I cursed myself. Of course, he was working. It was the evening on a weeknight. Aiden always worked. He loved his job. He would probably like it more if he didn't have a broken hand because of me, but that was why I was texting him.

Me: *Just checking on you.*

Aiden: *I'm fine. Just working. You coming in tonight?*

Me: *No. Just a quiet night at home.*

With my cats. But I didn't say that.

Aiden: *Violet and Harmony are here. So you wouldn't be alone.*

Always worried about me. But I was good at being alone.

Me: *I'm good. Long day. Have fun cooking wings.*

Aiden: *Fuck you and your wings.*

I smiled. I loved buffalo wings. And Aiden hated them. Aiden liked adding fancy things to the wings and making them glorious. And I totally agreed with that and liked it. But that didn't mean I couldn't razz him about it. But then I remembered he had been hurt because of me, so I didn't. Instead, I just texted:

Me: *Anyway. Have fun. Got to go. Night.*

Aiden: *You need to talk?*

Crap.

Me: *I'm fine. Night.*

I turned my phone down and turned it over so I wouldn't have to look at the screen. And then I just shook my head, wondering what was wrong with me. Why was I like this? And why, after all this time, did I still have feelings for him?

I shouldn't. He wasn't mine. I needed to remember that.

He wasn't mine. He had never been mine. And the sooner I got that through my skull, the better for both of us.

CHAPTER SIX

AIDEN

"ARE you *sure* your hand doesn't hurt?"

I bit back a nasty retort and inhaled deeply through my nose while rolling my shoulders back. I had to remember that despite the kid asking me the same *damn question* every thirty minutes or so, I was actually enjoying myself.

And lashing out and beating him senseless for worrying about me wouldn't be productive.

I swear to God, I sound like Brendon right now.

"I'm fine." I held up my injured hand and shook the cast in the air as the hustle and bustle of the kitchen around us kept moving. "I'm not even using it. You're the one doing all the chopping and slicing." I narrowed my eyes. "And the more you ask me about it, the slower you are at prepping for tonight's meal." I sing-songed the last part, and Dillon winced before going back to slicing up onions.

I didn't usually do all the prep like this since I had staff to do some of that for me before I even showed up. But I had peeled my fair share of potatoes in my day, sliced onions, peppers, and other assorted vegetables and fruits.

Food prep had been where I started, even before I had gone to dish duty. I had started in food prep at the house and then had found a dishwashing position when I was sixteen. That had led to other jobs.

Dillon was working on prep today, while I was showing him the ropes. Yeah, it was pretty much nepotism at this point, but we weren't in a five-star restaurant, we were in a bar that I owned. The three other cooks that I had working in and out of the kitchen didn't care. The kid helping out meant they didn't have to do prep. My sous chef had stepped up into my position, and I was doing a little bit of everything where I could. Plus, they all liked Dillon.

I didn't know if they actually liked me, but I really didn't care.

They just had to listen to me and deal with the fact

that, yeah, I changed the menu often. There were some staples, but then there were things I liked to add.

We were a bar, but we weren't the bar we used to be.

The brewery we used to be had been failing. There were too many just like us, and it didn't matter that we had the family history and the fact that Jack and Rose had made this place so great.

Things had changed, and so we'd had to change with them. We hadn't taken away what Jack and Rose had done to make it special, but we had added a few things.

Like my tapas.

And my daily, weekly, and seasonal menus.

It had taken a couple of months, but the people in the kitchen had finally started having fun with it. And that meant I didn't have to yell as much.

Even though I kind of liked yelling.

"Okay, so what are these onions going in again?"

"We're mincing them, so they're going in a lot of things. In a base for our sauces, we're going to sauté them for a few things, and part of this is going in the salsa that we're making for the nachos. Everything's fresh here, nothing pre-chopped or canned."

"Wait, some people just open up a jar of salsa at a restaurant?"

"Yeah, I know, it's a disgrace."

"Or it could be the fact that it works for them and it's

part of the bottom line," Jorge said as he walked by, snorting.

I flipped him off and went back to helping Dillon.

"We are not those restaurants. What they want to do is fine. But I will not have that in my place of business. Do we understand that?"

"Yes, chef," they all said at the same time, and I just shook my head.

"I'm starting to believe you don't actually mean 'yes, chef' when you say it," I said dryly.

"I have no idea what you mean," Beckham said as he walked in, carrying an empty crate for bar glasses. "I mean, I don't actually call you *chef*, but I could if you want." Beckham winked, and I flipped him off.

I kind of missed being able to use my dominant hand to flip people off, but I was getting better at using my left hand to do it.

"You don't call me chef because I'm not in charge of the bar area."

"Lame," Beckham said, walking back towards the bar with a filled glass crate. "I mean, come back with better comebacks."

"I would, but all of my time and energy is focused on the kid here."

"Don't blame me for the fact that that was really crappy."

I glared at the kid, who just shrugged.

"What? I'm starting to think maybe you hit your head rather than just your hand."

"You're lucky you're on the clock so I can't beat the crap out of you."

"Another dollar for the jar," Beckham said dryly. "Every time we threaten with violence, we have to put a dollar in the jar."

"At least it's not cursing," Jorge said. "Because that would fucking suck."

I just shook my head and put a dollar in the jar. All of us threatened each other jokingly, but we knew if anyone else heard it, we'd get our asses handed to us. And not in a violent way. So, we were trying to do better about it. I just sucked at it sometimes.

Also, I was pretty sure half the dollars in that jar were mine. We didn't actually know who the money was going to in the end. Probably all of us for beers. Or maybe we'd donate to a charity or something. Sandy, one of my line cooks who wasn't here today, usually took care of it. She was the only one any of us trusted with the money. Mostly because she wasn't going to spend it on herself.

But still.

"Okay, let's get back to it," I said as I gestured towards Dillon. "Once I'm out of this damn cast, I'll be back to my brilliant menus."

"Oh, good, he's going back to his brilliance," Jorge said, laughing.

"Yeah, I mean, it's been like a whole minute since he started talking about that beautiful, brilliant mind of his when it comes to food," Beckham said, coming back into the kitchen with an empty tub.

"Don't you have somewhere better to be rather than here, razzing me?" I asked, glaring.

"Well, Brendon isn't here, so I can't make fun of him for his bartending skills. I'll just have to make fun of you and your attitude. That's sort of my thing."

"I thought your thing was to be the brooding, quiet guy behind the bar?" Dillon asked, his attention on his hands rather than anything else.

I lifted up my fist, and Dillon held his up. We fist-bumped, and the kid went back to work.

"Good one," I said.

"I hear the girls talking about his broodiness all the time. I figured it was good to put it into conversation."

"I do not brood," Beckham said.

"Really? I think out of all of us in this building, you brood the most."

"Well..." Dillon said and then trailed off. "What?" he asked after I'd glared.

"What do you mean by that?"

"Well, all you guys pretty much brood a lot. Until you

get laid. And then there's not so much broodiness or swaggering. And that gets annoying after a while. You, however, brood a lot. Maybe you need to get laid."

"He is my favorite Connolly brother," Beckham said, grinning. "Seriously, favorite Connolly brother."

"You know, I'm pretty sure we're going to need to hire a new bartender soon," I said dryly.

"You would think that. But you would be wrong." Beckham just stomped out, indeed brooding on his way. If the man wasn't razzing one of us, he was actually brooding. Dillon had it right.

"Okay, enough of this crap," I said after a while. "Let's get through the rest of the training, that way, more time will pass, and my hand will heal so I can get back to what I love."

"You mean you don't love hanging out with me and teaching me all the mundane things that you hate?" Dillon asked, his voice all too casual.

I held back a curse. Not because of exactly what the kid was saying, but because of what he *wasn't* saying.

Because I hadn't been the best brother to Dillon. I had actually been a really shitty brother to Dillon at first. I hadn't even known about his existence until he was eighteen years old, and I had lost so much time because I had been an asshole. Because I had blocked all communication with my brothers.

And Dillon was the one who suffered from that. Yeah, we agonized too, but Dillon was the kid here. He was the innocent one.

And now he was trying to find his place with us, even as we tried to find our footing when it came to being a Connolly brother. We were getting better, but sometimes, we missed out on the stupid things because we weren't ready to take responsibility for our past actions.

"Hey, just because I'm going to be able to start using my hand again the way I want, doesn't mean you can just walk away from your duties. You're stuck back here with me, kid. I mean, yeah, you're a Connolly brother, but that doesn't mean you can just get away with not helping this place. You get me?"

Dillon's eyes widened for a moment and then filled with something that neither of us wanted to name right then. He gave me a tight nod.

"Yeah, I get you. So, does that mean I get to play with the frying pan at some point?"

"Yeah, maybe in a couple years."

"Oh, Aiden," he whined.

"Don't whine. Get back to chopping. If it's not good enough, I'm going to make you do it again. And you don't really want me to have to deal with waste, do you?"

"No, chef," Dillon muttered and went back to his work.

I just smiled and shook my head.

He was a good kid. And I was glad I was getting to know him.

I just hated the fact that it had taken so long to get to this point.

By the time we finished the prep and were getting to filling all the orders, Dillon was still working on some of the backend stuff while I was doing most of my work one-handed. I had gotten pretty good at it, even though I wasn't exactly ambidextrous. But you couldn't hold me back for long. Mostly because if I were held back, I would start to glower and probably break something in my house because I was a fucking idiot.

Not that I'd ever actually admit that to my brothers. There were boundaries, after all.

I let the rest of my staff work, knowing that they could probably handle most nights without me, but I didn't like to leave it alone. This was my place now. And I had my stamp on it. And I really loved what I did. I wanted to make sure that everything I did was worth doing, and that meant I was here, even when I was hurting.

Thankfully, my hand didn't hurt as much as it used to, but I was still a little tired.

I took off my apron, set it on the counter off to the side, and headed out to the front of the restaurant and bar.

Brendon and Cameron pretty much ran this area, and I didn't mind. I had my space, and they had theirs.

It was busy tonight, and for that, I was grateful. I could still remember the first month or so that I had been here, right when I was wondering if I was really going to quit my job and work here full-time. The place really hadn't been busy on a weeknight. And it wasn't as busy as it needed to be on the weekend either.

It had felt like a part of my childhood had died, the one that had been solid and pulled me through when everything else had sucked. It felt like death.

It wasn't that Jack had done a bad job, it was that he hadn't been able to do it on his own, and things had changed. He had been draining his life.

And we hadn't been there to help him. His sons hadn't been there to help him.

I would blame myself for that until the end of my days.

But we were here now, and the place was doing well. Beckham and Cameron were behind the bar, laughing and making drinks.

Brendon was helping the waitstaff, mostly because he liked being on the floor in a manager capacity when he wasn't in the office helping with everything that needed to be done paperwork-wise.

We each had our zones, and we were good at those. Mix them up, though? Yeah, we weren't the best.

But that's why we were brothers. We did what we needed to do and got it done.

I looked over to the far corner booth and smiled. I should have known who would be here. Because it wasn't a weekend night, it was a Thursday, and that meant people would be playing pool in the back, and my brothers' girls would be at their table.

I walked over and shook my head. "It's like you guys are just here for me and my cooking. You should have told me you were here earlier, I would have brought out something special." I leaned down and kissed the top of Violet's head and then the top of Harmony's.

They each gave me strange looks, but I shrugged it off.

I wasn't the best at showing affection, and I didn't really like touching people, but I was getting better at it. Because these were my brothers' women, and that meant they would be family one day. They were already practically family now.

So, I needed to stop being an asshole and get over myself.

Of course, as soon as I thought that, I looked over at the other two people in the booth.

I lifted my chin at Meadow and smiled. She gave a little wave back. She was one of their new friends, a neighbor of Violet's, and pretty sweet. I didn't know her that well and honestly didn't hang out with her that much. But it was good to see her again. She seemed to settle the other three somehow.

It was always a little jarring to see the three girls here and not see Allison with them, but I wasn't going to mention that. After all, they probably thought about it often.

And I had to wonder if Meadow thought about it, too.

Finally, I looked over at the fourth woman and nodded.

"Hey, Sienna. Surprised you're here."

I hadn't meant to say that, but it wasn't like I could take it back now.

"The girls wanted to come out. So, here I am." Her gaze moved down to my hand.

"You doing okay tonight?"

I looked at my hand and shrugged. "Doing fine. Dillon's doing most of the work. I left him alone back there with the kitchen staff."

"Poor Dillon," Violet said, laughing.

"No. My poor staff," I corrected.

"Dillon's great. You need to be nicer to him." Harmony smiled as she said it and took a sip of her drink.

"Me? I'm the nicest one of us."

"Really?" Sienna asked. I ignored all of their laughter.

"Really."

"The food was great tonight by the way," Meadow put in. "Thank you."

I looked down at each of their plates. It looked like they'd gotten the grilled fish and three salads. I studied what they'd left behind and hadn't eaten. "Yeah, Dillon helped with most of this. I did the rest of it. He's doing a good job. Looks like you enjoyed it all." I looked over at Sienna. "Didn't like some of the fish?"

"It was fine."

I straightened. "Just fine?"

She rolled her eyes and huffed under her breath, "Oh, stop it. I'm just not that hungry. It was really good. I wouldn't have gotten it here if I didn't know that it was going to be amazing. Fish just doesn't heat up well the next day, so it's not like I could bring home leftovers."

I fidgeted, and I didn't know why. "But it was at least okay? Better than okay?"

"You and your ego, Aiden," she snapped.

"I can't help it if you don't appreciate good food."

"Okay, that's enough," Violet said. "You don't want people to stare or run away from the bar. Go back to work, Aiden. We're just fine here. Thanks for checking on us."

I looked between the four of them and tried not to feel as if I had just been dismissed, even though I clearly had been.

Just because Sienna didn't want to finish her meal because she wasn't hungry or some shit like that, didn't mean she didn't like my cooking. I didn't have to take it so personally. Dear God, I needed some help.

I gave them a tight nod and walked back to the stockroom where I should have gone in the first place. I needed to pick up a few things, and I shouldn't have gone out to the front where looking at Sienna would just make me irritable for no good reason.

She made me a lot of things for no good reason.

I started piling things up in my hands and cursed at myself when I realized that I needed to take another trip because I didn't actually have two working hands right then. It made things a little more difficult.

I really wanted out of this damn cast.

I still couldn't believe I had fucking broken my hand on some asshole's face. I knew how to hit. I knew how to make a fist.

I just hit the man at the wrong angle because he had shifted right at the perfect time.

I still blamed that fucker's face.

"Here, let me help you with that," Sienna said from behind me. I turned abruptly, dropping everything to the ground.

"Motherfucker."

"I didn't mean to startle you. I'm sorry, Aiden. I keep saying the wrong things."

I looked up at her, wondering why the hell she was apologizing. She never apologized to me.

I frowned and then figured since she was here in this small room, it was time we talked.

So, I closed the door behind her and ignored her wide eyes.

"What is wrong with you?" I growled. Okay, not exactly what I wanted to say.

"What is wrong with *you*? Did you just lock me in here with you? What the fuck, Aiden?"

"You keep running away from me."

"So you're trapping me to talk with you? Really, Aiden? Are you that desperate?"

"I'm not desperate at all. But you keep running away. Why are you acting so weird? You never apologize to me. You never walk on eggshells around me. What's wrong?"

"I just offered to help you because you couldn't hold it all because your hand is broken. Because of me. So, just stop it, okay? Every time I look at you, I feel like it's my fault that you're in pain. I'm sorry if I don't know how to handle that."

Her words hit me like a ton of bricks, and I tried to control my breathing.

"It wasn't your fault, Sienna. Is that why you've been ignoring me? Because you blame yourself?"

"Just stop it, Aiden. I don't want to get into this right now."

"You never want to get into it."

I hadn't even realized I was standing right in front of her, her back against the door, our lips a bare inch apart.

Both of our breaths were coming in ragged pants, our bodies close, so close I could feel the heat of her, could almost feel the softness of her.

And so, I did the one thing I shouldn't. I let go of my sanity and took her lips.

The kiss was soft at first, and then it was hard and fast. She tasted of her drink and just Sienna. My tongue flicked against hers, and suddenly my free hand was on her face, arching her neck just enough so I could deepen the kiss.

I craved her, needed her touch, her taste, everything about her.

She was my addiction, my frailty, and even though I knew I shouldn't, I couldn't help but want her. Couldn't help but want this to last. To want this kiss to never end.

This was just like before. Like the one other time she'd let me have her. Let me touch her.

The one time I'd let myself be someone else.

The one time I'd given in.

And then her hands were on my chest, and I was taking a few steps back, listening to her.

Because I refused to be the guy who didn't stop. Who didn't back away.

"What was that?" she asked, her breath ragged.

"You know exactly what that was, short stack."

"It was a mistake. That's what it was."

I tried to ignore that lash, but I couldn't. "It was just like before. Don't you remember, Sienna? Don't you remember at all?"

She looked at me, her eyes wide, her face carefully devoid of emotion. "Before didn't work at all, did it?" And then she opened the door and left. I let her. I didn't reach out. Didn't ask her what she'd meant by that.

Because it *hadn't* worked out before. It hadn't worked for many reasons, and not just because of who we were.

Because of who had once stood between us.

It hadn't worked. And I had a feeling it never would.

CHAPTER SEVEN

Boys. There's just something about them that makes me want to love them and strangle them.

Not at the same time.

Maybe.

-Sienna, age 14.

SIENNA

BEFORE

"If you don't hurry up, we're going to be late," Aiden snapped at me, and I glared over my shoulder at him.

"You're the one who said that you wanted to drive me. That means you're going to have to wait on me. I had a long day, and I'm still not done with my hair."

"Seriously? Your hair. Could you be any more of a woman right now?"

That put my back up, and I stomped over towards him, my hair half dry, and only wearing a tank top and leggings.

I ignored the way his gaze traveled over my body. Yeah, I had curves, and he could just shut the fuck up about them. He didn't look at me that way because he wanted me. Aiden never wanted me.

There was a reason for that. I wasn't Allison. And that was just fine. I was getting over it.

Maybe.

Whatever.

"You did not just say that. Do not ever say anything like that again."

He held up his hands. "Sorry. Just slipped out. I swear, I'm not an asshole."

"Yeah, you are. You relish it. Usually not a misogynistic asshole, though." And it was hot because he wasn't cruel about it. I had issues.

"That is true. At least, I hope."

I just sighed and put my hands on my hips. "You do

get overprotective and growly, but I think that's just natural. Anyway, give me five minutes."

"There is no way you can get your hair and makeup done in five minutes."

"Oh, so you're saying I need to have my makeup on?"

He held up his hands, his eyes wide. "I'm not even going to touch that with a ten-foot pole. Don't try to trap me, woman. I know what a trap sounds like. And that was very much a trap."

I just smiled, snorting. "Okay, that was totally a trap. Sorry. I don't usually lay those out for you like that. Or anyone for that matter. That just seems wrong."

"And yet you did it anyway."

"It's just so easy with you."

"So you say. But, really, it's going to take you way more than five minutes. We're already late. They're probably going to start the damn pool tournament without us, and that means I'm going to have to deal with my brothers being pissed off at me for like a month. And I really don't want to deal with that. They're so fucking hormonal when they're pissed off."

I narrowed my eyes. "There you go again, making sexist comments."

"I am not." He paused. "Fuck. I am." He pinched the bridge of his nose. "I'm tired. And I don't want to deal with this pool thing tonight, but I don't really have a choice. Because it was Brendon's idea, and that means we have to make sure that everything goes perfect for him."

I tilted my head, staring at him. "What's up with you?"

"Nothing's up with me."

I took a couple of steps forward and put my hands on his arm. "Something is up with you. You're acting weird."

"I'm always weird, according to you."

"Yeah, but now you're weirder."

"Fuck you, Sienna."

I wish.

I let that thought run through my mind, and then promptly ignored it. There would be no fucking Aiden tonight. Or ever. He was my late best friend's ex-boyfriend. There were rules. And one didn't poach. Especially when everyone was still grieving.

I already felt like an asshole for always wanting him. Even when I shouldn't. I really wasn't going to want him right then.

And it didn't matter that he got even hotter when he was acting all broody and angry.

It really wasn't fair.

"Aiden?"

"What?"

"Aiden."

"Fine. I don't want to do this tonight. I don't particularly like playing pool, but it's helping the damn bar. And it was Brendon's idea, so we have to go for it."

"Is the thing that's annoying you the most the fact that it was Brendon's idea?"

"No."

"Aiden."

"Every time you say my name, you keep yelling it. As if I'm supposed to just magically know what you mean by it."

"You do. Aiden."

He threw up his hands. "Fine. Everybody's all into this whole pool night or whatever. And yeah, it's working, but they keep giving me shit over my stuff. And, yeah, I'm acting like I'm fifteen rather than my age, but it annoys me to no end that I get ragged on, and they're doing just fine."

"But they're not."

"Excuse me?"

"You all razz each other. But you're all doing something to help the bar. You're doing great things. I loved it before, and I kind of wish it could have stayed that way, but it couldn't, not in this economy. Not in this city. You guys are changing things but keeping the same flare. And your food's amazing, Aiden. I loved it when you cooked at your old restaurant, but here? When you're surrounded by family, and it's a little more low-key? I love it even more."

He studied my face, frowning. "You went to LaFleurs?"

I shrugged. I hadn't actually meant to say that out loud, but now, I couldn't back away. "Yeah. A couple of times. It was a little too pricey for me, so I could only go like on a date or if it was like a celebration."

"But you went to LaFleurs. Where I worked. And I didn't know. How the fuck did I not know?"

"I only knew you worked there because your dad mentioned it once or twice." Or forty times.

Jack really loved his sons and made sure that everybody knew that. So, he had mentioned a few times that Aiden worked at LaFleurs as a line cook, and then as a sous chef. And that he was doing freaking amazingly. And so, I had wanted to go. Meaning, I'd scraped up the change in my couch and then used a credit card to pay for it, but it had been worth it. Possibly some of the best food I'd ever had in my life. "The food was great, Aiden. You never have to worry about that."

"How do you know I'm the one who cooked it?"

"I don't, but you probably had a part in it. However small it may be."

"Hey. There's nothing small about me."

My eyes widened, and I did my best not to look down. It was kind of hard not to because it was sort of the thing in the room just then.

"Really, Aiden?" I tried my best not to sound like I was too interested. Because I was. But I wasn't.

"Sorry. Force of habit. Anyway. I didn't know you came. To LaFleurs that is." He winked. I rolled my eyes. "I wish you would have come back to the kitchen or something. Or sent a note to say that you were there. I would have liked to see you."

"I thought it might be weird. It had been a while since we had actually talked to each other. You know? Friends just sometimes move in different directions for a while."

"We're not moving in different directions now. I guess you're stuck in my life for a while."

"Aw, I guess you're stuck in mine, too."

We both grinned then, and I realized that I was still watching him and that we were close. Too close.

And I was only wearing a tank top without a bra. I could feel my nipples hardening against my cami, two pinpoints of arousal just screaming to anyone that looked that, no, I wasn't cold, I was very turned on in Aiden's presence.

Damn him.

"This is a really bad idea," Aiden muttered.

I only had a few moments to figure out exactly what he was saying before his mouth was on mine, and my arms were around his neck.

His hands were on my ass, molding me to his body,

and I could feel the hard line of his erection digging into my belly.

Bad idea? No, the worst idea.

The worst idea ever.

Aiden had been in love with Allison. And Allison was gone.

Yet here I was, humping her ex-boyfriend.

I was going to hell. A special hell for best friends who were the worst friends.

With Aiden's mouth on mine and every single teenage dream of mine coming true, I couldn't focus.

So, I pushed Allison out of my head, even though it was the worst thing I could possibly do, and just felt.

Aiden arched into me, rocking his body. I let him, moaning into him as I clung.

I was wanton, needy, and I never wanted this to end.

There was no talking, no need to. No need to tell each other that we were making a mistake, that we should stop.

Because we already knew that. He'd already said those words. And I agreed.

There was no need to repeat it.

Instead, I leaned my head to the side as his mouth latched onto my neck, sucking, nibbling, taking a gentle bite. His hands molded to my ass, squeezing as he rocked his cock against me.

Suddenly, I was on the floor, the breath knocked out

of me as he was on me, pulling my cami up slightly so he could kiss my belly.

"You're so fucking soft," he growled.

"More," I muttered. "I need more."

His beard was rough against my skin, but I didn't care. I would likely have beard burn, *and* rug burn. Along with everything else that burned between us.

And I didn't care.

I just wanted more.

And then he was above me again, kissing me roughly, his hands in my hair, and then one hand lowered, tugging my cami down so my breasts popped out. And then his mouth was on my nipple.

He flicked and sucked. And I writhed.

This was everything that I'd thought it could be. Everything and more.

I needed to stay out of my head.

I just needed to be in the moment. A moment that seemed like just a dream. This wasn't really happening. It couldn't be. Because if it was really happening, then it would end, and then I would feel everything again.

Aiden tugged my cami strap down, pinning my arm to my side, and then his mouth was on my other breast. Suddenly, I wasn't thinking about the aftermath anymore.

Instead, I was wrapping my legs around him, wanting more, needing more.

Just more.

More.

That was the only word that kept coming to mind, over and over again.

More.

"Aiden," I gasped.

"I'll make you come, make you come hard. And then I'm going to be inside you. You want that, Sienna? All that fighting, all that anger you have towards me? I have it, too. But all I want to do is fuck you hard. And I'm going to do it for you right against this floor. Until we're both spent yet still needing. What do you say?"

"You talk a lot, Aiden. Why don't you just get with the action and show me that cock of yours?"

His eyes widened for a fraction of a second, and then he laughed before kissing me again.

He had my clothes off in an instant, and then he was kneeling between my legs, his eyes wide. "You weren't wearing panties."

"I was going to put them on. Later."

"Don't on my account."

And then his head was between my legs, his mouth on my pussy.

I arched into him, wrapping one leg over his shoulder and a hand in his hair. He kissed me down there, licking, sucking, spreading me so he could spear me with his tongue. And then his mouth twisted on my clit, and I came, shouting his name.

But he didn't stop there. He kept licking, sucking, fingering me with two fingers, and then three. I clamped around his digits, coming again.

Somehow, he had found that magical spot, the one that only my fingers and different toys could find.

He was a fabled one, one who actually could find that spot.

And I hated him for it.

But I needed more.

And then I was tugging on his shirt, pulling it off as I kissed down his chest, sucking on one nipple and then the other.

He muttered under his breath, reaching into his wallet for something, and then he was throwing off his shoes and tugging off his pants.

I only had an instant to look at that long, thick, glorious cock of his.

It was hard, ready, and I wanted it inside of me.

"Holy shit," I muttered, and then Aiden smiled at me.

I loved that smile of his.

He didn't do it enough.

And I wanted him to smile.

Now, he was smiling at me.

All naked and about to be inside of me.

I pushed those scary thoughts out of my head because I just needed this moment.

I wasn't going to have this moment again.

"I love the way you look at me."

"You're going to love it more once you're inside me," I snapped, and he laughed.

And then he was over me, one hand under my thigh, pushing my knee up to my face, the other at the base of his cock as he slammed home.

I was pretty sure I saw stars at that moment. He stretched me, filled me to the brim, and I couldn't hold back my grunt, or even suck in a breath.

This was everything. Everything I hadn't thought I needed.

His mouth was on mine, sweat pouring down both of our bodies as we tried to pause for a moment.

And then there was no more thinking. No still moments.

Just hard and fast and ready.

He slammed into me, over and over, our hands all over each other, his between us, making me come once, twice, a fifth time in the moments that we had with each other.

I hadn't thought it was possible.

But Aiden fucking Connolly made it possible.

With each pound, with each thrust, I slid farther

along the rug, and I knew my ass would have rug burn at the end. I didn't care.

I just wanted him.

And I had him.

And then he was shouting my name, slamming into me one more time, and we both froze, his release aching, loving.

No, not loving.

This wasn't love.

This was Aiden fucking Connolly.

And he was still inside of me. Hard, yet not mine.

He lay on top of me for a moment, trying to catch his breath as I did the same. His forehead was on mine, but he wasn't looking at me.

It was all I could do not to look at him.

And when he slid out of me, I closed my eyes, swallowed hard, and rolled to find my pants.

He must have done something with the condom and pulled on his pants because then he was coming back, tucking himself back into his jeans. I just sat there, trying to put on my cami.

"Sienna."

I shook my head. "We're not going to talk about this. You're not going to talk about it again. You're just going to go, and I will meet you at the bar later. Because we can't do this again. We're not like the others."

I met his gaze then, and his face shut down, just like I needed it to.

Because I had just slept with my best friend's ex-boyfriend.

And she wasn't even here for me to face her.

I was the worst sort of person.

And as he walked away without a word, I wanted to tell him to come back.

I wanted to tell him that I loved him before this and that I was afraid I would love him more after.

But I didn't.

Because there were no words.

I had broken the one oath that friends make with one another.

And Allison wasn't here for me to do anything about it.

CHAPTER EIGHT

AIDEN

Now

The feeling of deep release was a satisfaction like no other. The fact that I was looking at my bare hand, able to slowly move my fingers, was an orgasm in itself.

Not that I was going to tell the nurses or doctors that were staring at me exactly what was going on in my mind.

But considering the fact that I now had my cast off after almost six weeks, it made me feel as if everything was as exactly as it should be.

"Okay, tell me what you're feeling," the doctor said. I looked up at her.

"Uh, great. Thanks. Can I go now?"

She just raised that very penciled-in brow at me, and I winced. "I guess I can't?"

"No, Mr. Connolly. You can't yet. Let's talk about exactly what you're not going to do. And what you are going to do."

"Okay," I said and then sighed. I settled back into my chair, looked down at my now free hand, and knew it was going to take a while. I wouldn't be able to just go back to the kitchen and start chopping and dicing and sautéing and doing everything that I was actually good at.

Instead, it seemed, I was going to have a lesson.

I had hated school before, and I really wasn't a fan of it now.

"You were very lucky with the breaks in your hand. If they had been any worse, we would've been talking about surgery, loss of sensation, hindered dexterity, and worse. You hit that man's face at the exact wrong angle when you already had some carpal tunnel issues because you use your hands too much."

I blinked. "Carpal tunnel?"

"You're going to have to do better. And I'm not just talking about with your job. It's disturbing the number of people who are coming into different offices at this point because they have carpal tunnel thanks to their phones and just using their computers to scroll. The way you hold your phone will have to change. You'll also need to move it from hand to hand. I noticed that you already had it in your left hand while we were waiting to take off your cast, and that's good. But, the less you hold it, the better. Because you'll be holding it at the bottom corner, right at one of your fracture points, and that will have to change."

"Really? My phone is what caused me to break my hand?"

"Not exactly. But it didn't help. We see these types of injuries all the time. Not necessarily the breaking, but the stress to your ligaments and other parts of your hand. We see them in smaller boys and teenage boys, as well."

My mind went straight to the gutter, and from the way she narrowed her eyes at me, I had a feeling she knew exactly what I was thinking.

"No, Mr. Connolly. Although that probably doesn't help the situation. I was talking about video games. With the rise in video games and cell phone usage, our hands are becoming weaker. Now, I'm not saying that you broke your hand because of the way you hold your cell phone or your knife at work. And you have so much muscle memory in how you hold your knife at work doing what you do that you're not going to be able to change that overnight. If ever."

"I don't know if I'm ever going to be able to do that. I hold it exactly the way I should after years of training."

"And that's great. But it's the same motion over and

over again, even the way you hold a frying pan. And I know you're an amazing chef, but you're going to have to take care of your body."

My brows rose this time.

"An amazing chef?"

She just smiled. "I know that you worked at LaFleurs. I've had your food there. And I've been to your bar. Good food. And I know that all the changes you put in have been for the better. But we're not talking about that right now."

"Good. Because I'm not changing the way I cook."

"That's fine. It's just going to be harder for you to get back into the swing of things. That means you're going to have to do some physical therapy."

I cursed, and she just looked at me, giving me a bland look. "Are you done yet?"

"I could probably go longer."

"Anyway, physical therapy is a must. Because while I have a feeling if you really think about it, you can change the way you hold your phone and even the way you use a computer, you're not going to be able to change the way you cook. That's ingrained in you at this point. And as much as I'm going to tell you to *not* do it the same way every day, it's just going to happen. But you need to be realistic. In order to make sure your hand is as strong as it can be, that means physical therapy. I have a few people in mind for you, and I can refer you. But you need to do it. If you don't want to get another stress fracture by just like chopping something, you're going to need it."

"Physical therapy?"

"Physical therapy."

I frowned and looked over the list that she gave me, shaking my head. "There's one not on this list, a friend of mine. Can I see if she can help?"

"A friend?" she asked, her tone dry.

I shook my head. "Not a friend like that. An actual friend."

Okay, so that wasn't entirely truthful. I continuously thought about our one afternoon together, the one where my knees still ached because of the rug burn—and I knew her ass had to have some marks, too. Yeah, that one. The one that we didn't talk about. We hadn't talked about it before the attack, and we sure as hell hadn't talked about it since.

So, yeah, Sienna was my friend. It was just harder to remain friends when we weren't actually talking about it. Considering that I didn't like talking about my feelings, the fact that I was even thinking about that was saying something.

"Is she a massage therapist, or a physical therapist?"

"It's Sienna Knight. She's a sports therapist, so almost exactly the same thing, but I'd rather work with someone I know. Plus, I'm sure I could actually fit into her schedule because we know each other."

"I know Sienna Knight. She's one of the best at what she does. She also has a long waiting list to get into her rotation. She doesn't exactly do what you need, but she's trained." She looked at me a moment before nodding. "If you can fit into her schedule, I'll make it a referral for your insurance."

"Sienna really is the best, isn't she?" I asked, and the doctor gave me another of those looks.

I really was acting out of character, and I did not like it. There was just something about Sienna that made me act weird.

"Let's see what we can do," the doctor said, and then we went through exactly what my aftercare things would be.

Thankfully, by the time I got out of there, I was ready to go back to work, new hand and all.

I called Sienna right away. When she didn't pick up, I hoped she was just at work and not avoiding me. The phone beeped, and I left a message.

"Hey, my cast is all off, but I need physical therapy. I can go to someone else, but I'd rather do it with you. Mostly because you know me. What do you say? Will you help a guy out?"

I hung up. I was a little nervous. What if she didn't want to help me? What if she didn't want me in her life at all? It was weird because all I could think about was that kiss in the stockroom. And her other kisses before. I'd had a crush on her before, just a little one when we were younger. But then I'd started dating Allison, and Sienna had just become my friend. It was all complicated, but then again, all of us were.

We had so many connections within the group, and it was sometimes hard to remember where one person began, and the other ended.

But I wanted things to get back to normal. I wanted to go back to my kitchen, I wanted my brothers to get off my back, and I wanted Sienna and me to get back to our normal fighting and laughing with one another. I didn't like the fact that things were awkward. Maybe us working together on my hand would make things better.

My phone dinged, and I looked down at it.

Sienna: *At work. But have your doctor send over the info. I'll see what I can do.*

I smiled. I knew this had to be the answer. Things would change.

They had to.

"OKAY, you're getting better, let's see your mobility."

I looked up at Sienna and grinned. "Yeah? You want to see my mobility?"

She just rolled her eyes and then glared at me. "Really? You're here as my patient. That means there is no flirting or fuddy-duddy stuff. That is strictly against the rules."

"It is not. You're doing this as a favor to me."

"A favor, maybe. But you're still in the books. And that means it's wrong."

"I don't want to be right," I said, laughing as she glared at me again.

"What is wrong with you? You're acting all weird."

I shrugged and then followed the exercises she gave me, rotating my wrists, gripping the ball, doing everything that I could so I wouldn't end up losing the strength that I had in my hand.

I didn't know why I felt weird. Why I was acting strangely. Probably because every time I was around Sienna now, I couldn't help but want to be near her more. I liked making her laugh. I liked when she yelled at me. I liked when she lost her temper and got all red in the cheeks and bit her lip when she didn't know what to say because she was too angry to put words together.

I loved all of that. And I had missed it recently. Yeah, it had been because of the attack in some ways, but we had been acting weirdly ever since we slept together. And we hadn't talked about it. We needed to.

I didn't like that things had changed. And not for the better. I didn't know exactly what I wanted, and I didn't know if I would know that until I had it. But I did know that I missed having Sienna make me laugh. I missed having Sienna anger me like no other. I just missed her.

That was why I was in physical therapy with her. Even though I probably should've gone somewhere else.

"Okay, then," I said after a moment. She looked up at me and groaned. "Today will be our one day together. I'll do the exercises you tell me to, and then I'll find someone else. That way, it doesn't get weird. Because you're feeling weird. You look it."

"You're an asshole. Did you just say I look weird?"

"Do you always tell your patients they're assholes?" I asked, my voice very prim and proper.

"No, I don't. I just mean this is a mistake. I was just trying to help you, because..." She trailed off, and I cursed.

"Don't you dare tell me that you were trying to help me because you feel guilty about me breaking my hand. Because it wasn't your fucking fault, Sienna. Get that through your head."

"Shut up. You can't tell me what I'm allowed to feel."

She let out her breath, rolled her shoulders back, and

looked like she was calming herself. "I'm not going to raise my voice in my place of business. There are other people outside of this office, and I cannot act like a crazy, insane person. You're just making me feel that way. So, why don't you find that other physical therapist? This will be our one time, and I'll make sure you get the help you need, but this is the one time we'll be in this office together. Is that understood?"

I looked at her and then nodded. "That's understood. I won't bother you again. But, Sienna? I'm here because I miss you."

I hadn't meant to say that, and it didn't even sound like me. By the look of shock on her face, she agreed.

I shook my head quickly. "You know what, forget I said that."

She swallowed hard and looked at me. "I don't know that I can. I miss you, too, Aiden. But things are different. I guess they're always different. I don't know what to say, Aiden. But I don't think I can be your physical therapist."

I winced and nodded. "Yeah, I can see this was a stupid plan. I guess I just thought of you at the time I knew that I needed someone to help me. You know?"

She nodded and smiled. "Well, I am pretty good at my job."

"You're the best at your job, according to my doctor."

She smiled then, and it actually went to her eyes this time. "I've always loved Tracy."

"Tracy, is it?"

"Yes, Tracy, a happily married woman with four kids."

I blinked. "Four kids. How in the hell can she be a doctor and have four kids?"

"Because her wife carried all of them, and she actually spends time at home instead of only at the hospital. I really don't know how she does it. She's a goddess. All of us strive for that status."

"Four kids," I said, shaking my head. "That's scary. Know what's scarier?" I asked.

"What?"

"I have a feeling there will be more Connolly kids coming around soon."

"Oh, yeah. Violet and Harmony are total breeders."

"Oh, yeah. The way that Brendon and Cameron look at them? I have a feeling that engagements are on the way if they haven't already been secretly done."

"Oh, Violet and Harmony would tell me. Even if your brothers don't tell you."

"That's probably true. But you'd tell me, right?"

"If I was engaged?"

My heart stuttered for a bit, and I wondered what the hell that was about. "No, if someone got engaged and they told you. You'd tell me?"

She bit her lip and then shrugged. "Probably. Because the guys probably didn't tell you or because they thought they already had. Or you just weren't listening. So, yeah, if one of our friends get engaged, and you don't know, I'll be sure to tell you."

"Good."

We stared at each other for a minute, and then I cleared my throat.

"Anyway, I'll find a new physical therapist. But, Sienna? I don't want to go back to the way things have been. I want to talk to you. I like hanging out with you. I like yelling with you. It's fun."

"You know, we're very weird. Because I missed the yelling, too. I'm just not very good at anything these days without yelling at you."

"I find that hard to believe."

"Maybe. But, sure, let's hang out more."

"And we need to talk."

Her eyes narrowed. "We're not talking about that."

"The storage room? Or your house?"

"Neither."

"You know, I think we should. Because I think it wasn't what happened in the alley that pushed us apart. So we need to talk."

"You hate talking about your feelings."

"I know." I threw my arms up into the air, careful not to actually injure my hand. She glared at me. "See, what's wrong with me? I'm worried about my feelings and your feelings. That means, we need to talk it out so I can get over it. Can't you see that this is stressing me the fuck out?"

Laughter danced in her eyes, but her face was very stern otherwise.

"Aiden."

"Don't *Aiden* me. Tell me."

"I think we need to finish this up, and then I'm done for the day."

I held back my sigh, knowing that I needed to get things back to the way they were, but there was something more. Because we needed to talk, and she wasn't going to do that in her office. Which I knew.

"I'll walk you to your car when we're done then."

"Thank you." The fact that she didn't stop me, didn't say that she would be fine, worried me. She had to still be scared after the attack. If me walking her to her car like I should've done that night would help at all, then I would do it. Because Sienna was my friend. And I refused to see her hurt again.

As soon as we were done, we headed out to the parking lot, and I walked her towards her car. We didn't say much, mostly just talked about our families. And I didn't touch her, I kept a safe distance. Mostly because I felt like if I were to touch her right then, she'd jump out of her skin. She was still so damn afraid, even of walking out into her own parking lot.

And that worried me. We'd already talked about enough that day though. I'd bring it up again later. Or I'd talk to Violet. Hell, for a guy who hated talking, I was sure doing a lot of it.

We were just to her door when she froze.

I froze with her and looked around.

"What?" I whispered.

"Do you hear that?"

"What is it?"

"It sounds like a little kitten. A meowing sound."

She was off then, and I was chasing after her. We ended up near one of the bushes right by the front of her car, and then she went to her knees, squealing. "Oh my God, Aiden. It's a little kitten. Doesn't even look to be a couple of months old." She reached out, and the mewling stopped before I could stop her.

"Stop. You don't know if it could hurt you."

"It's a kitten, Aiden," she snapped over her shoulder before she went back to look at the cat. "It's okay, baby. Here, let Auntie Sienna help you."

Before I could help her, she was straightening with a little ball of white and gray fluff in her hands. "Oh, look at her," she whispered.

"Her?"

"Or him. I'm giving it some privacy. I don't think there're any other kittens around. We would hear them or see them. But let's take a look. I cannot believe someone just left him or her out here."

"Or the mama cat left it out here. Could be feral."

"No, I don't think so. Look at her. She's been well taken care of, at least until now."

I let out a sigh and then helped Sienna to her feet as she curled the kitten into her chest.

It looked at me with big, wide eyes, and I couldn't help but want to reach out and pet its head.

So, I didn't.

I wasn't against cats per se, but pets and I didn't usually mix. Mostly because I'd never had one.

Couldn't have pets when you were in foster care, and Rose had been allergic to cats and dogs. So, we hadn't had them.

Sienna and I searched for more cats, calling out for them, and all the while, she curled the little kitten against her chest.

"I think it's just this one. Just the little baby in my hands."

"Okay, what are you going to do about it?"

"What are *we* going to do about it? The answer is we're going to the vet, and then if this little baby needs a home, she's going home with you."

I froze, blinking at her.

"Excuse me? You're the one holding it. You're the one who found her. I'm not taking that baby home with me."

"Oh, yes you are. I have four cats at home already. Four very stable cats that would not be happy to have a little baby kitten that they would either be scared of or territorial about. Plus, I'm already the cat lady at the store. I cannot be a fifth cat, cat lady. However, you have all that space, and I will totally help you. I just can't disrupt my house right now with a kitten. We'll just go to the vet and make sure that he or she is fine, and then we'll get you everything that you need. I have a feeling you're going home with a cat, Aiden."

"I am not going home with that cat."

"Bet you."

I narrowed my eyes. "Bet me what?"

"I don't know. But if this little kitten needs a home, I can't take it, so that means you have to."

I narrowed my eyes and gritted my teeth. "Fine," I said and then smiled. She took a step back, probably a little wary of my smile. She should be. "We'll take the cat to the vet. If it needs a home, I'll take it home."

Her eyes widened, and she smiled.

"But," I said quickly before she interrupted, "only if you go on a date with me."

CHAPTER NINE

There's nothing a glitter cannon can't fix.

-Sienna, age 26.

SIENNA

"I'M GOING on a date with Aiden tonight," I whispered, looking down at Runway on my chest. "I cannot believe I agreed to go on a date with Aiden!"

Runway glared at me for daring to wake her up, and then settled more firmly on my chest as the three other cats on the couch either played with each other or purred.

I was the cat lady with a date, and I had no idea how it had happened.

We had gone to the vet, and the vet had said the kitten was okay, it just needed a home. And Aiden had offered to take him home. But only because he had somehow gotten the agreement out of me that I would go on a date with him. How had that happened? I still didn't know. It shouldn't have. I was not going on a date with Aiden Connolly.

I sighed.

I was totally going on a date with Aiden Connolly. And I was probably going to hell on top of it.

And I was losing my damn mind at the same time. All of that had happened the day before. And that was why I was currently sitting on my couch, surrounded by my cats, watching another episode of *My Little Pony*. Because there was nothing a glitter cannon couldn't fix. And Pinky Pie, the little, pink pony with the bright pink hair and a case of ADHD most likely, made me smile. Because I was seriously losing my mind, and I needed something that didn't make me think, that just made me smile.

Because I wasn't supposed to go on a date with Aiden Connolly.

Aiden had been Allison's. And, yes, I had slept with him, but that had been a mistake. We had both agreed that.

Okay, we hadn't actually talked about it to make a firm agreement, but it had to be the case. Because he had loved Allison. He didn't love me. We were just friends.

We'd just slipped and fallen into each other. Over and over and over again.

Yes, that was totally what I could say.

I really needed a drink. Or another episode of *My Little Pony*. That would make me feel better.

I still couldn't believe I was going on a date tonight. With Aiden.

This was such a mistake, but I couldn't back out now. He knew where I lived. And he had taken little Diego with him.

Aiden had named the kitten Diego. Instead of Little Fucker, like he had wanted to.

I didn't know how it had happened, but somehow, I was doing the one thing I'd always wanted to do, even though I knew it was the one thing I never should, and Aiden now had a little kitten at home.

A sexy man with a beard and a growl while holding a kitten?

There was no way I could say no to that.

There was something seriously wrong with me.

I had no idea what I was doing tonight.

Because this wasn't just a normal date.

This was a date with my best friend. Or, at least one

of my best friends. The guy who used to date my best friend who was now gone. And the guy I'd already slept with once, though we hadn't actually talked about it.

To say this was complicated would be a freaking understatement.

I looked down at Danger and Moxie, who were currently cuddling to the point it was almost indecent.

But I would let the relationship go because they loved each other, and just the fact that they ignored me while they were cuddling didn't mean they didn't love *me*.

I looked on my other side as Baby played with her tail, then looked at me quickly before looking back at her tail as she tried to nibble on it.

This was my life. I worked in the morning, I worked in the afternoon. I worked out afterwards, I ate dinner, and then I hung out with my cats. Occasionally, I would hang out with my sister and Harmony and even Meadow. But I didn't go on dates.

I used to, but then I just got busy and tired.

And if I were honest with myself, no one was Aiden.

And that was on me. Nobody else.

"Do I need to call the girls?" I asked Runway, who finally just shook her head and shrugged off me. That sent the other cats into a tizzy, and soon, all four were running around the house before eventually finding different places to lay down.

That left me alone in my living room with *My Little Pony* on the screen.

I shook my head, sighed, and turned off the TV.

I needed to shower and get ready for my date. And figure out exactly what I was going to wear.

And decide if I was going to tell the girls.

Did I tell Violet and Harmony and Meadow that I was going on a date with Aiden? What would they think? What would they say?

I didn't think any of them knew that I'd ever had a crush on him, not even when we were younger, and it had been more of a thing.

I wasn't great at hiding my feelings, but I thought I was decently good at this.

Mostly because I'd had to be. Because it was just sad to long for your friend's boyfriend. So, I hadn't.

I pushed those feelings from my mind and had found other boys to date and other people to be in relationships with. And I had never told Violet or Harmony or Allison what I felt for Aiden. I was afraid that I would have to tell Aiden at some point. But I couldn't. Because if I did, then it would be a thing. And I couldn't let it be a thing. We were just going on a date. Like friends.

Friends who'd had sex.

Really good sex.

So, I couldn't call the girls.

I let out a laugh, telling myself I was making the right decision when the doorbell rang.

"It's not that late," I said quickly, looking down at my phone. No, I still had a couple of hours until my date with Aiden. So, who would be at my door right then? I didn't really know anybody that just showed up. People usually texted ahead of time.

Maybe it was the UPS man. I did order enough packages from Amazon that I should probably own some stock or something.

I went to the door and opened it, and then froze.

"You really didn't think you'd go on your first date with Aiden without us, did you?" Violet said as she pushed past me. Harmony leaned forward and kissed my cheek as she did the same, and then Meadow just gave a little wave and skipped past me.

"What? What?"

Every time I said the word *what*, it got louder, a little sharper, a little more shrill.

"Well, we got here exactly at the right time," Violet said, tapping her chin as she studied me. "Because there's no way you can go on a date with Aiden looking like that," she said as she gestured towards me.

"I mean, she's not even wearing a bra," Harmony said, clucking her tongue.

"Unless that's what she wants because a no-bra thing could totally work," Meadow said, and the three of them laughed.

I barely resisted the urge to cover myself, knowing that I was wearing a very thin t-shirt over no bra because it was right after work and I felt like being lazy.

"I'm going to repeat myself. What are you three doing here?"

"We're here to help you get ready for your date, silly," Violet set down her bag and then put her hands on her hips. "First, you're going to have to take a shower. Then we're going to go through what you're going to wear and how you should do your hair and things. This is going to be fun, isn't it? I love first dates." She started clapping her hands, and then Harmony just laughed.

"No, you don't. You like dating when it has to do with Cameron. You hated first dates. Do you remember how jittery you got with your first date with Cameron?"

"You want to talk about dating?" Violet said, leaning towards Harmony. "We can talk about all of *your* first dates."

"We are not going to go through that list. My first dates with anyone other than Moyer or Brendon were horrendous."

I just looked between them, blinking. The fact that

they were all staring at me, talking about their best first dates and knowing I was about to go on a date with Aiden didn't make any sense. This couldn't be happening.

"Are you okay? We could leave," Meadow said quickly.

"We will absolutely not leave," Violet said. "We are here because we love you. And because this is a big deal, even though it's not a big deal. We're not going to make it a big deal, even though it might be a big deal."

"I really don't understand your logic right now," I said, looking at all of them.

"You don't have to understand our logic, you just have to get all ready and look pretty and have a wonderful time tonight."

"This doesn't make any sense. How are you even here? I didn't tell you."

"I know you didn't tell us," Harmony said. "And that hurts." She put her hand over her heart and gave me a mock glare. "It truly hurts."

"Oh, shut up."

"Don't tell her to shut up." Violet raised her chin. "I know why you didn't tell us. Because you think it's weird. Because you don't want to make it a thing. But, of course, it's a thing. And hiding it doesn't help anyone."

I looked at my sister and then at my other two friends. "It's a thing. Did Aiden tell you?" Would Aiden actually tell my sister that he was going on a date with me? That didn't seem like it could happen, but considering that I was going on a date with Aiden, all other things seemed to be out of my hands and a little weird.

"No, Aiden told Cameron when Aiden asked for the night off, and I heard it from my boyfriend."

"Do you have to say, 'my boyfriend' like you're sing-songing it? Like you're in a high school musical?" I asked, trying to get my thoughts in order.

"I will say 'my boyfriend' as much and however I want to. Because it's kind of fun. And you are going on a date with your boyfriend."

I held up my hands. "Aiden Connolly is not my boyfriend. It's just a date. Just a dinner and a game between friends. And I'm really just going because he held a kitten hostage."

The three of them looked at me, blinking.

"I'm going to need some more information about this kitten," Meadow said softly.

"Well, we found a kitten. His name is Diego. He's cute. But I couldn't bring the little guy into my house because, you know, the clowder."

"Yeah, four cats is already two cats too crazy."

I flipped my sister off. "Oh? Are you going to tell the other two cats that they have to leave? Which two would you take from my home? I thought you were their Auntie Violet."

"Oh, stop it. You know I love those cats like they are my actual nieces and nephews. I helped fill their stockings this Christmas. But that is beside the point. You can't get a fifth cat. And adding a kitten to your house would just be too much."

I threw out my hands. "I know. Hence why I told Aiden that if he couldn't stay at the vet's, he had to stay with Aiden. And Aiden got all grumpy like he usually does and growled at me. But then he got like this weird light in his eyes and said that he would totally take the kitten if and only if I went on a date with him. A kitten's life was in the balance. I couldn't just say no. That is why I'm going on a date with Aiden Connolly. To protect Diego. Nothing else."

They just looked at me and then burst into laughter.

"I can see the laughter. I can hear it. I do not appreciate it."

"Oh, we're not laughing at you."

"I'm not laughing. Therefore, you're laughing at me, not *with* me. You can't actually finish that statement." I threw my hands up into the air again and started pacing. Baby ran into the room, bumped my calf, and then ran back out. My cats were weird, but I was weirder. I even had a t-shirt that said that.

"Okay, go shower, because you stink."

"Fuck you too, Violet."

"Oh, you're going to shower, you're going to shave your legs, you're going to shave whatever else you need to, and you're going to look fuckable for that man of yours. Because you are going on a date with Aiden Connolly, and you're going to have a fucking good time."

I blinked at Violet and then looked at Harmony and then Meadow. "That seemed very harsh just then," Meadow said, looking between all of us.

"Very much so. Are you okay?" Harmony asked.

"My sister is about to go on a date with my boyfriend's twin. It is all very soap opera, and I've been waiting for this."

I just stood there. "Waiting?"

"Not only is this out of one of my favorite books, I've also looked at the way you two tend to not look at each other or look at each other too much. I've noticed the way you two fight and get all growly at each other. You guys are perfect for one another."

I held up my hands, trying to stave off everything. They didn't even know I actually had a crush on him or for how long. It was just getting to be too much. "Okay, you're going to have to slow your roll, because I am going on a single date with Aiden. And, yes, the fact that you are dating his twin makes it weird."

"Imagine the double dates," Violet said, clasping her hands together and getting a faraway, dreamy look on her face.

"Excuse me, triple dates. I'm also dating a brother." Harmony put her fists on her hips and started laughing as everyone else burst into giggles, as well.

Everyone but me, that was.

"Okay. I'm going to go shave my legs and my underarms. But nothing else."

"Well, if that's what you need to shave, that's what you need to shave," Meadow said very seriously. But I saw the laughter in her eyes, and I cut her from my friend list, as well. I cut them all.

"I'm going to open some wine."

"Oh, good idea, Harmony. But we don't want to get her too drunk. I'm sure she'll get drunk enough when she's on her date," Violet sing-songed, and I turned away from all of them.

They were traitors. All of them were traitors.

I stripped down in my bathroom and shoved myself into the shower, cursing myself as the cold water blasted me because I'd been too impatient to actually wait for the water to get hot. I scrubbed and shaved and nipped and tucked and growled the entire time.

I didn't know why I was so out of it. This was just a

date. Just dinner. I had been out to dinner plenty of times with Aiden.

Never really alone, but this wasn't any different than usual. Right?

I turned off the water and pulled the shower curtain back, only to scream like there was an actual man with a butcher knife coming at me.

"Really?" Violet said dryly. "You're going to scream like that movie? I'm just in here looking through your makeup. And I guess you really didn't shave everything," Violet said, giving me a wink before handing me a towel. "Oh, don't look like a prude," she said as I tried to cover myself. "Sienna, what is up with you?"

I wiped the water out of my face and covered myself with my towel. "You were standing in my bathroom, and I didn't know you were here. Of course, I'm going to scream, you pervert."

"Oh, shut up. I wasn't actually expecting you to throw the curtain open like you were ready to show everything to the world."

At that moment, Harmony and Meadow came running in, each holding something different. Harmony held a wine bottle, while Meadow held a spatula.

"We heard screaming," Harmony said.

I looked at Violet and threw my head back and laughed.

I used the edge of my towel to wipe my tears and just shook my head. "First, the fact that it took you this long to get back here after my scream...we need to talk about that. Second, you're not going to actually come back if you hear screaming, right? I would call 911, maybe. And a wine bottle and a spatula? Not really the best weapons."

Harmony just shook her head at me. "It was what we grabbed in the moment. At least we came for you. I mean, we could have run away and just left you and Violet to your own devices so you could be chopped up into little bitty bits and put into a trash bag never to be seen again."

I gave her a bland look and then looked at Violet. "We need to stop letting her watch so many true crime shows."

"She has that podcast, as well," Meadow added. "I actually really like it."

"Anyway, I'm all nice and clean. I'm going to do my hair and my makeup, and then I'll be ready to go."

"I'll get the wine. Oh, and I made a little tiny charcuterie board," Harmony said. "I couldn't help it. You had all the fixings."

She shrugged and went off to the kitchen, Meadow following her.

I just looked at Violet and wondered what the hell I was doing.

"If you don't want to go on this date, you can tell him. Aiden's not that much of an asshole."

I smiled at her and sat on the toilet seat in my towel, letting my hair drip water down my back and my shoulders. "He's an asshole, but then so am I, sometimes. But he's also kind of sweet. And, yeah, I could have said no. I could have found a different way to get Diego into Aiden's house or found him another home. But I said yes."

"And this is your first date with him?" Violet asked. I looked up at her, frowning.

"Yes."

"So, you sleeping with him didn't count as a date?" she asked, and I started.

"Huh?"

"I know you and Aiden slept together."

"Did he tell you that?" I asked, standing up.

"No, you did." She sighed and grabbed my hands. "With your face, Sienna. I can tell when you sleep with a guy. You guys have been acting so differently around each other, and then things got weirder after the attack. I kind of laid off wanting to talk to you about it because I knew we had more important things to worry about. But now, you're going on this date, and I just want you to be happy, okay? If this isn't what you want, then that's fine. You don't have to do this, pretty. You can walk away, and everything will be fine. And I'm going to tell you something very similar to what you told me when I was going on a date with Cameron."

I bit my lip, not really wanting to hear.

"You're allowed to be a part of this group and want something for yourself. You're allowed to try this date and see if this new connection can work. If it doesn't? We will figure out what happens after. But you can't hold yourself back for fear of what could happen, and for fear of what we might think. Because I can see your excitement under all the nerves. So, go out tonight and have fun. And just remember that you are loved. No matter what happens, we're always going to be here for you. Okay?"

I hadn't even realized I was crying until she was wiping the tears from my face.

"Now, let's get you all prettied up. Not that you're ugly right now," she added, and I punched.

"Ow."

"What? I'm just getting ready for dinner and a hockey game. There's a lot of fighting at those."

"Only Aiden would take you to a hockey game for your first date."

"I like sports. It's a thing."

"It's your thing with Aiden. And I love it. Now, I'm thinking jeans with cute rips, a very cute top, and a leather jacket with flats. But the flats that cover more of your feet than just the normal ballet flats because it's going to be cold in there. I would go boots. If you want. Maybe the ones with the cute buckles. But you have those sparkly flats that are just perfect for dates in case you go for a drink later."

"Well, why don't you just set out my clothes for me like you're Mom."

"Oh, I could totally do that."

I laughed, took the glass of wine from Harmony, did a toast with my friends, ate some cheese, and got ready for my date with Aiden Connolly.

Because Violet was right. Even though this was my first date with Aiden, this was really just a date. It was just a meal and a game with a friend.

If things were going to change—and things had already been changing without my doing anything as it was—maybe I needed to take care of my own destiny.

Or maybe I just needed to go with it for once.

By the time the girls had left, I was all coiffed and in the boots with the buckles because my feet did get cold at hockey games.

And four minutes before Aiden was supposed to arrive, the doorbell rang, and I sucked in a breath.

I didn't know why I was so nervous. I had been to sports games with the Connollys before. Just not actually with Aiden.

And not by myself.

So, when I opened the door and I saw him there in jeans that were tight around his thighs, a t-shirt that clung to his chest, and that leather jacket that just made him look all bad boy and sexy, I almost threw myself at him.

Would it be wrong if I were to climb him like a tree?

"Dear God, short stack," Aiden growled.

I looked down and held back my laugh since my boobs were really out in my top, thanks to Harmony and Violet's help with picking out my bra and shirt.

"You look nice," I said, my voice a little too high-pitched.

"You look fucking edible. And that's going to be a problem. Because I'm probably going to want to hit some-body again." He held up his hand. "And I'm not in the mood to find a third physical therapist."

I just leaned forward and rested my forehead against his shoulder, my own shaking with laughter.

"We are really bad at this whole thing," I whispered.

He ran his hands down my hair, careful not to touch the top. "Well, I guess we should practice. Maybe it'll make us a little better. And did you see? I didn't touch your bangs. Last time I did that, you gut-punched me, and I'm not in the mood for that."

I leaned back and laughed. "Okay, then."

"I'm going to take that as a good sign," Aiden said, and then he kissed me.

Just a soft kiss, just a brush of lips, and I knew that I'd be okay. Because all of the thoughts of anything but

Aiden's lips and what we could do tonight just for fun flew from my mind.

This was just a date. This was just Aiden. This was just me.

And maybe it was okay to fall, just this once.

CHAPTER TEN

AIDEN

"IT'S like you know me or something," Sienna said with a wink as we made our way to our seats in the stadium. The Avalanche were playing the Red Wings, and it was a rivalry my brothers and I loved more than most. Even though none of us knew when it had actually started.

I put my hand on the small of her back as we found our row, and she just grinned over her shoulder at me.

"Well, I kind of do know you. I guess that could be a good thing, right?" I asked as we took our seats, careful not to jostle our beers.

"I guess it can be a good thing. Or it can be a horrible

thing because we already know too much about each other, and this is really just a terrible mistake." She said the words so quickly that she winced after, and I just shook my head.

"Okay, let's not go there. Shall we?"

"Well, I did sort of say yes because you were threatening a kitten," she said with a wink, and the couple on the other side of her gave me a weird look.

I pinched the bridge of my nose, glared at Sienna, and then looked past her at the big, tattooed man and his curvy date. "I wasn't actually threatening the kitten."

Sienna grinned and turned towards the couple, putting her back to me even though I knew she was laughing at me at the same time.

This woman.

"Well, he did say that he was just going to let this poor kitten stay at the shelter instead of taking it home and caring for it if I didn't go on a date with him. Don't you think that's pressure?" I looked down at her and scowled.

"That is not how it happened." I squeezed her shoulder, and she squirmed in her seat, though I didn't let her go. I didn't want to stop touching her, even if I knew it was probably not the best thing for me.

"That is totally how it happened." She looked at me, winked, and then turned back to the couple. "I mean, I probably eventually would've said yes if you would've just, you know, not threatened a poor wee little kitten."

She was laughing then, and the couple gave us an even weirder look, but then smiled.

"Okay, I can totally tell that there's a story there, but I'm a little freaked out," the woman said. "By the way, I'm Olivia, this is my husband, Derek."

Derek lifted his chin, and I did the same. "Now, should we report you to animal services?" Derek asked, and I sighed.

"No. Because I was going to take the kitten no matter what."

"You were?" Sienna asked, turning so she faced the ice but could still talk to all of us. "Oh, by the way, I'm Sienna. This is Aiden."

"Hi," Olivia said, the light in her eyes dancing.

I held out my hands, trying not to look like I was a kitten killer or something. "I was really going to take the kitten. Diego. As we named him. But I really just wanted to talk, hence the whole using the kitten to my advantage. But I wasn't going to just let it stay out in the street crying like that." I looked up at Derek. "I'm rarely home, but when I am, I now have a kitten on me. And if I could actually bring the little thing to work, Sienna would probably create like a knapsack for me or something."

"Oh my God, can I make you a knapsack?" Sienna

asked, putting her hands together beneath her chin. "Just imagine the little baby kitten in a little sling across your chest. All the swoons."

Olivia laughed and gave Sienna a high-five. "Seems like totally all the swoons. But you'd probably have to beat women off with a stick if they saw him with that."

"Hey, I'm sitting right here," Derek said, wrapping his arm around his wife and giving her a firm kiss on the mouth. "Don't talk about swooning over another man."

"Aw, you know I only swoon after you, boo."

"Boo?" he asked, laughing. "We're not going with boo."

"Oh, boo. I'm so sorry that you're afraid of a cute little nickname."

"Okay, keep at it, and next time, our little game is going to be a little less subtle when we're at the hotel," he glowered, but I could see the laughter in his eyes. I wondered what the hell these two were talking about. Because from the way Olivia blushed, the two apparently had a story to tell.

"Excuse us," a deep voice said from the other side of me. I looked over at two college-aged guys who already looked like they'd had one too many beers yet still had another in their hands as they tried to find their seats.

"Yeah, dude, I think you're in our seats," the one with the glassiest eyes slurred.

"No, I think we're in the right spot. What seat are you?" I asked, shielding Sienna just a bit. Derek was thankfully already standing so I wouldn't be alone in case these guys started trouble.

"What the fuck does it matter? These are our seats," the drunkest man said.

"No, these are ours, but if you show me your ticket, I'll try to help," Sienna said from around me. I shifted just slightly so she wouldn't get within view of the asshole.

"What the fuck ever, bitch," one of them grumbled, then pulled out his ticket and glowered. I took a step forward, pissed off and ready to hit the smug son of a bitch, but Sienna put her hand on my elbow, stopping me.

"Whatever," the dude mumbled. And then he stomped off to the row in front of us and they took their seats.

It was only because Sienna was holding me back that I didn't punch the shit out of him for calling her a bitch.

"Don't," she whispered. "I'll make sure I accidentally kick their chairs all night, but this is our first date, and we're going to have a good time. Okay?"

I narrowed my eyes, then gave her a quick kiss on the lips that surprised us both.

"I should say something," I whispered. "He doesn't get to call you that. No one does."

"No, he doesn't get to ruin tonight. Okay?"

"He does something else, I'll deal with it. But no one gets to call you that, Sienna. No one."

She cupped my face and looked at me with warmth in her eyes.

"Thank you. Now, let's have our own beers, and watch the Avalanche maybe actually beat Detroit. Hopefully."

"From your mouth to God's ears," Derek said from behind us, and we all laughed, the tension easing out.

The guys in front of us didn't look back, but they did keep drinking. A lot of drinking. I may own a bar, but I didn't drink as much as most people might think. I had one beer and called it a night. I wanted to drive Sienna home, and frankly, I wanted to keep my wits about me because I didn't trust the guys in front of us.

The Avs got the puck at the first spray, and we cheered, screamed, and cursed out the opposing players for a clear icing that hadn't actually been called. I loved sports, loved almost every sport out there, except for golf. I'd tried to get into golf, I even attempted to learn how to play, but I just couldn't deal with the motions.

Maybe when I got older, I would figure out what was so great about the sport.

"I'm so glad that we're here," Sienna said, grinning at me. She'd had just the one beer as well, and was now drinking water, but she was still bouncing and dancing along to the music during each of the breaks.

"I'm glad I could get tickets."

"These are pretty good seats for last minute. How on earth did you get them?"

I leaned over and kissed her temple. It was nice to just kiss her, keep touching her as if I had the right to do so. She didn't back away, and constantly wrapped her arm around my waist if we were standing or put her hand on my knee when we were sitting. "I have my ways."

"Sure, you do. Are you sure Diego is fine alone?" she asked as the ice girls came out with their little shovels to scrape off some of the ice.

"Dillon's stopping by to feed him and hang out with him. I'm pretty sure the kid and Diego are best friends at this point."

She smiled widely at that. "So, he has a key to your house and everything? That's a big step."

I shrugged as if it weren't a big deal, even though it was. "I gave it to him a couple weeks ago. Mostly because the other brothers already have a house key, so I wanted to make sure that he had one, too. Plus, if I didn't, I was pretty sure that Cameron or Brendon would've just done it to get it over with."

"It's good that it's the four of you now, not just the three of you, you know?"

I squeezed her hand, swallowing hard. I didn't like the ball of emotion in my throat. I didn't like to feel much of anything.

"I'm figuring it out. Probably a little slower than the others want me to, but I am."

Sienna just shook her head and leaned into me. "You're doing it on your own time, and you might've been an asshole before, but you aren't now. You're allowed to have your own reactions, and you're allowed to figure out what you need."

I just looked down at her in awe. Everyone else thought I was an asshole for the way I had treated Dillon when we first heard about him. And for the fact that I hadn't known about him for far too long because I had cut ties with Cameron. Yeah, Brendon had done it too, but I was pretty much the one who had done it first. Because I had been pissed off at my twin for leaving me, for abandoning me for our addict mother. And it didn't matter that I thought I had been in the right. In the end, I had been wrong. All of us had. And Dillon was the one who'd been hurt because of it.

But we were learning. Somehow.

We got to the end of the second period, the Avs down by one but doing pretty well considering, and we both decided to get up and get something to snack on. Derek and Olivia came with us, as did the drunk guys in front of us. We went the opposite way from them, maybe out of instinct, or perhaps just because we didn't want to deal with the guys who had been screaming throughout the entire match and practically spilling beer on one another. I didn't know why they were still allowed to be there, but whatever. I wasn't going to let them ruin my date.

"So, how long have you two known each other?" Olivia asked, leaning into her husband. "And I'm totally being nosy. Sorry. I heard you say 'first date,' but it looks like you're friends, too."

"Olivia," Derek whispered, kissing the top of his wife's head. "You don't have to know everyone's histories. And you should know that more than anyone." He winked at her, and she blushed.

Seriously, this couple had so many layers that I kind of wanted to figure them out, but Derek was bigger than me, so I wasn't going to ask. The fact that he was a tattoo artist with full sleeves and could probably bench press me was not lost on me. However, I knew where I was going to get a tattoo the next time I needed one. I'd heard good things about Montgomery, but the fact that I now knew one of the artists was probably a plus for me.

"We've been friends since we were in high school," Sienna said, looking at me. "Seems like forever."

"Yeah, it kind of has been."

"And this is your first date? Oh, how sweet," Olivia

said as she clasped her hands in front of herself. "But I'll stop asking more because you're both looking a little awkwardly at me, and I realize I'm a little pushy."

"I think I just found a new friend," Sienna said, looking up at me before going back to talk to Olivia. I just met Derek's gaze, and we each shook our heads.

Apparently, our women were going to be fast friends, and the fact that I had just said "our women" was a big step for me. I had asked Sienna out for more than one reason, but it had been so I could talk with her. So I could figure out exactly what was going on inside my mind. But we weren't acting like this was a first date. Because maybe it wasn't. We'd already had sex—very, very good sex. We'd already been through a whole hell of a lot together.

So, while this might be our first actual date, I felt like we'd had more than just this one moment.

Derek and Olivia went off to make a phone call after we got our snacks, and I stood in the waiting area with Sienna for a bit. That way, we didn't have to go straight to our seats. There was something I needed to say to her, and while this probably wasn't the best time, I didn't want to keep it down for too much longer. I had a feeling if I did, it would get weirder than it already was. I seriously wasn't any good at this whole relationship thing. Hadn't been since Allison, and it was showing.

"Hey, Sienna? There's something I need to tell you."

"Oh?" Sienna asked. She looked a little worried, and I held back a wince. I really wasn't good at this.

"So, I know this seems like a first date, but there's something that you should probably know." I let out a breath. Just do it fast, and it's not a big deal, right? "Back when we were in school before I started dating Allison, before we all became the group of friends we were, I had a crush on you. And it seems silly in retrospect to even mention it, but I wanted you to know that it wasn't just that one night at your place. It wasn't just me asking you out and using a kitten to get it done. I just thought you should know."

She blinked, and I just stared at her. She had frozen at the mention of Allison's name, and I knew that was something else we needed to talk more about. Because no matter how much time passed and what happened between us, Allison would always be here. And that was something we needed to work through.

"I guess I should tell you that I had a crush on you, too," she said, her voice small. "More so before you started dating Allison, and then I pushed it away because it didn't matter. You were with her."

A sharp bark of a laugh escaped, and I ignored it when people looked at me. Relief and confusion slid through me. There was so much between us, and we just kept ignoring it. Except now. Now, we couldn't. And maybe that was a good thing. I wasn't like Brendon or Cameron, who were good at talking about shit. But I was learning. "We are something, aren't we? Because I thought you didn't like me, thought that you didn't want anything to do with me, so..."

"So you went out with Allison," Sienna said, her voice a little wooden. "And I was just a little shy, so I didn't say anything. But Allison wasn't shy."

"No, she wasn't." I swallowed hard. "And I can't regret being with her, if that makes sense."

This was seriously not the place or time for this, but I didn't want to stop, not now that we were talking.

"I get it. I really do. And I guess we need to talk about that, too. But maybe not here."

I reached out and cupped her face. "Yeah, not here. But we will. I probably shouldn't have brought it up here, but I've never been great at timing."

"Timing? What's that?"

I leaned down to kiss her, but she darted forward at that moment, rapping her forehead against my chin. I cursed and looked down at her pale face.

The drunk dudes that had been in front of us for the whole game were smirking at her, standing far too close for comfort, and I clenched my jaw, anger radiating through my body.

"Hey, no wonder you want to tap that ass. Feels kind of nice."

"Don't you dare touch me again," Sienna growled, her voice a little shaky.

"The fuck is wrong with you?" I asked, taking a step forward as I gripped the man's shirt. His drunk face paled just a bit, but I still saw the smirk. I fisted my hand at my side and winced, just remembering at that moment that I had just fucking broken that hand from punching a man.

"Aiden, just let it go. Just stop. Please?" I looked over at Sienna, aware that people were all around us but just looking at her. She was shaking, her body rigid, her face pale. And then I knew that it wasn't just me thinking about the last time I had punched someone. She was clearly not over the assault, and I was just making it worse. Like I always fucking did.

"Fuck," I growled and let the man go. "You better back off. Just go."

The little dipshits ran away, and no one really seemed to notice what had just happened. Everyone was worried about their sports and all that other shit, and here I was, making things weird.

"Can we go home?" Sienna asked, her voice emotionless. "I think I want to go home."

I reached out to touch her, but she flinched. And

that's when I knew that maybe I had fucked up. Again. Like usual.

"How about we go see Diego, and then I'll take you home?" I knew she needed space, but I also didn't want her to be alone until she wasn't so pale.

"Okay," she said with a sigh. "I'd like to see Diego."

And then she reached out and took my hand, my non-injured hand, and we left the game, not knowing who might win, but knowing that our night was probably over.

I had fucked up, but so had those guys. Sienna would normally be the one to stand up for herself and kick the guy in the groin or something, and the fact that she hadn't, worried me more than it should. Or maybe it didn't worry me enough. I didn't know, but it was something we needed to talk about. I just didn't know how to bring it up.

We didn't talk on the drive back to my place, just let the music play as things got a little more uncomfortable.

She just stared out the window, her hand thankfully on mine as I drove. I didn't mind driving one-handed, and I counted the fact that she was still touching me as a win.

When we got to my house, and I let her in, Diego came running out and jumped on Sienna's leg. She lowered to a seated position, picked up the little kitten, and rubbed her face on the little guy's head.

"You are seriously the cutest little thing I've ever seen," she said, her voice soft.

"He's a menace, and I should probably keep him somewhere safer than just in my house roaming about. But he learned how to open the door to my bedroom, so there's really no way out of it."

She looked up at me then, smiling, even though it didn't reach her eyes. "How did he do that? He's tiny."

"He sort of stretched from my dresser over to the door, and since I have the handles that go up and down rather than circular ones, I'm kind of screwed. So, he has free rein in the house. We are installing child locks on my cabinets, though."

"He'll probably figure that out, and then you'll just be the one having to deal with opening cabinets and hurting yourself. Especially with that hand of yours. Believe me, I know. Four cats, remember?"

I sat down next to her in the middle of my foyer and just looked at her.

"I'm sorry. Sorry for reacting the way I did. I should've talked first, reacted second. But those guys just blew my temper. And I think that's a problem. But I'm sorry."

She looked down at Diego, petting the little purring ball of fur and raising him up to her chin. "I'm fine. I guess I'm just not over it."

I wasn't either.

"Do you want to talk about it?"

"No." She said it quickly, and I held back a curse.

"But maybe you should."

She was silent for a moment. "Maybe you should, too."

"Maybe."

We were silent for another moment, just sitting next to each other, not touching. Diego's purrs were loud enough to rattle the windows, even though he was so tiny.

I didn't know how to fix this, didn't know how to make things better.

But then again, I didn't know how to fix myself.

I hated that this had happened to her, and there was nothing I could do about it. Because trying to protect her, at least physically, just seemed to make things worse.

We sat there for a few more minutes until Diego fell asleep, and she handed him over to me so she could stand up, take the cat back, then put him on his little bed on the couch.

She tucked him in, kissed the top of his furry little head, and then looked at me.

I swallowed hard and then walked the few steps between us so I could kiss her softly.

She melted into me, and I held back a sigh of relief.

We could still do this. We could still make this work.

At least, I hoped so.

"Let me take you home," I whispered.

"I think that would be best. But, Aiden? I'd like to do this again."

I let out an audible sigh. "Oh, thank God. Tonight didn't end the way I wanted. But I want to take you out again. I want to figure out what *this* is."

"Okay," she whispered.

And then I kissed her again before we walked back out to my car and I took her home.

She frowned at the mailbox when I pulled in, and I turned off the engine, looking at her. "What's wrong?"

"The flag's up, and I don't remember putting anything in."

The hairs on the back of my neck rose, but I shook it off since it made no sense. "Let me check it with you," I whispered.

"I'll be fine, it's just a mailbox."

"And we've seen enough movies to know it's never just a mailbox."

"Touché."

But we walked to the receptacle together, and she opened it as I stood in front of her. "It's just a rose. Weird, though."

I frowned, that tingling sensation not leaving me. "Why is someone leaving a rose in your mailbox?"

"This is the second one, actually."

"Excuse me?" I looked around as if someone were

watching us, though it couldn't be anything like that. I thought of her attackers, but they hadn't known who she was and hadn't taken her purse, so they didn't know her address. It couldn't be that.

"It must be my neighbors. They're really sweet and have left me baked goods on my doorstep in the past, you know? They knew I was hurt, and it's super sweet of them to make sure I'm okay. That must be it. I'll thank them tomorrow."

It didn't sit well with me, but Sienna didn't seem worried. Considering that we had been stressed out for the last half of the evening because of our own irrational fears, I figured this was just fine. It had to be fine. So, I walked her to her door, kissed her again, and waited for her to click the lock shut before I went back to my car.

But I couldn't help but look at the mailbox.

I couldn't help but wonder why someone would leave a rose. According to her…again.

CHAPTER ELEVEN

Asking for help sucks. Not asking for help is suckier.

-Sienna, age 10 after failing her science project.

SIENNA

THIS WAS NOT my first time on this couch, and I knew it wouldn't be my last. I looked around at the tan walls, and dark furniture, and the hanging photos that were of nothing and yet calming at the same time. Nothing was too bright, too bold, too sad, or too *anything*. It might have seemed bare to others, but I knew Mary did her best to ensure that the office was soothing and welcoming.

It didn't make it any easier today, however.

There was a rustling of paper and fabric against leather. "So, Sienna, how about you tell me a little bit of what you've been up to since I last saw you."

I looked up at Mary and tried to smile. I liked Mary. I respected her. But it was hard to smile. Hard to cry. Hard to do much of anything when I didn't know what to feel.

It had been at least six months since I last saw her. And I knew I probably should have seen her far more and sooner, considering everything that had happened over the past few months. But it was easier to tell myself that everything would be fine, that there was nothing wrong. That I could just talk with my friends and talk about myself. That I was totally healthy and doing great all on my own.

But that wasn't the case.

Considering what had happened the weekend before with Aiden? Not even close to being the case.

"I'm sorry for spacing so long between visits. But I thought I was doing okay." I *was* okay. But what *okay* meant for me had changed.

Mary just gave me a smile and nodded.

"Don't be sorry about asking for help. And don't be sorry for thinking you're okay. Because you don't need to talk about everything with me. I'm here to listen. I'm here for you to tell me what you need to. I'm not here to pry. I'm not here to strip all of your secrets. I'm just here."

"And to think I used to come here just for anxiety." I said the words casually, and she just smiled at me. A smile that wasn't condescending but just told me that I wasn't alone.

It didn't feel like she was placating me, only that she was really here to listen. And I needed to get back in the habit of actually allowing someone to hear me.

"I told you in my call before I came about Allison..." I let my words trail off, unsure of what else to say.

"I know. It hasn't been that long since it happened. We can start there if you'd like."

She looked at me, and I forced myself to look away. Instead, I looked at the billowing curtains as they swayed in the breeze from the ceiling fan. It was hard to put into words what I felt. Probably because the aching numbness that had been there when I first heard that Allison was gone hadn't completely gone away. Instead, it'd just festered to the point that sometimes I felt *everything* through the numbness, though not often enough.

Even when I'd been held against the wall with that man's hands on my throat, I'd *felt* something...but when I thought back to it, I couldn't pinpoint every sensation, every breath, every emotion. It was as if I were looking through a bubble and I couldn't quite figure out what I needed to feel.

That was why I was here.

That and Aiden.

Because Aiden knew I needed to talk about it. And I was afraid to talk about it with anyone else.

Would I talk to him about it?

I didn't know.

I wanted to.

He'd told me that he had feelings for me before...and I didn't know what to make of that. Then I'd blurted the same to him and yet...yet it wasn't the same. It couldn't be the same. Because we were already past the part where we were. Where things could go back.

"Sienna? Talk to me about Allison."

I pushed those thoughts away and thought of my best friend. Then it all came back.

"I want to know why. I think I'm at the angry stage of grief. Because I just want to know why she did it. And then it makes me feel selfish because it's not about me. It was about her. And all the signs that we missed. And the fact that she's gone and there's nothing I can do about it."

"That is a lot in very few sentences. Why don't we talk about it?"

"I just don't understand. But maybe if I was supposed

to understand, I would have understood before it happened."

"You can't change the past, Sienna. You can't fix something that's already happened."

"I just didn't see it. She was unhappy, and now she's gone. And there's nothing I can do."

"Having someone you love take their own life is hard on many, many levels. Not having answers is something that you're going to have to work through, and it may always be there for you, but I know you have a wonderful support system."

"Allison had that same support system."

"Yes, but I don't know Allison, she wasn't my patient. If she had been, this wouldn't be something we could talk about. I don't know what drove her to take her own life. I don't know why she didn't leave a note. None of us have those answers, but I'm here for you right now. I'm here for the answers that you can have. And to figure out how you're feeling right now."

"I'm angry. I'm sad. I'm pissed off. I'm just devastated. She was my best friend. I know Harmony and Violet are my best friends too, but Allison was my person. She was my person, and she's gone."

"Why don't you tell me something that makes you happy about her. Just one memory."

"When I was younger, I couldn't figure out exactly

how to put on my makeup the way I wanted. There weren't exactly YouTube tutorials for that back then, even though I'm not that ancient," I said with a laugh.

Mary just raised a brow, and considering she was a little less than a decade older than me, I should probably watch my step.

"So, every time, I ended up with dark raccoon eyes instead of the perfect smoky eye, and Allison would come over and fix it for me. Because she knew exactly how to do it with ease, with a smile."

"Go on," Mary said, and I did. I told her about dances, how Allison always knew how to make us laugh and was the life of the party. And we just talked.

I had talked about Allison often with my family and with the Connollys. We were all still grieving, but we were moving on. My sister and Harmony had fallen in love, and all of us were trying to figure out exactly how to make things work without answers. We had packed up Allison's home and had broken down while doing it. But we were human. And now we needed to figure out exactly what to do.

"Why don't you tell me what else is on your mind?" Mary said after we had talked about Allison for a little bit. We only had an hour to speak, and I had *a lot* on my mind.

"I also told you about the attack," I said quickly. Mary

leaned forward and nodded. She didn't touch me, and for that I was grateful. I wasn't afraid that Mary would hurt me, but it just reminded me of the man's hand on my throat, and even that guy's hand on my butt at the game.

"I just feel so stupid about how it happened."

"It's not your fault. You were prepared, but sometimes being prepared isn't enough. That's something that we all come to realize. Why don't you tell me exactly how you feel right now?"

"That I need to be stronger."

"That's not always the answer, Sienna."

"Then I don't know what the answer is."

"So, we can talk about that."

"It doesn't help that everything's all connected. The fact that Aiden blames himself, but it's not his fault. He was just going to get his phone. And I should have been safe. I wasn't. And then he got hurt because of me."

"Sienna."

I held up my hand. "I know it's not rational. But that's what my brain's thinking. And that's why I need to talk it out. That's why I need help. And you know I hate asking for help, but here we are."

"Your hands fist at your sides and you play with lint on your knees when you say Aiden's name. Let's talk about that."

"I went on a date with him," I said quickly. "I went on

a date with my dead best friend's ex-boyfriend. The same ex-boyfriend that got hurt because he was trying to protect me from people who wanted to take my money and whatever else they could in that alley. So, yeah, it's complicated, and I have no idea what to feel. And then these guys got drunk and touched me at the hockey game, and Aiden got angry. He gets so angry these days, and he got angry, and then I got scared, and he backed away. And it just pisses me off because I can't control what I'm feeling. I can't control anything. And I just don't know what to do about it anymore."

Mary looked at me and then nodded, taking notes. So many notes.

"You love him."

It wasn't a question, but my eyes widened, my heart speeding up just enough that I knew she could tell. Mary saw everything.

"I've loved him as Aiden Connolly since I was in high school. That love isn't the same as it was then, and it's not the same now. He's part of my life, even though there were times when he wasn't because that's drama and family and how people move apart. I don't know if I'm making the right decision dating him. But it's hard not to want to be with him even if I know it might be wrong, even if I know it might be too complicated. He makes me happy. Even for those few moments, he makes me smile."

Mary smiled then and nodded. "Then that's a start. Let's talk some more."

And so we did, we talked about Allison, the attack, and Aiden, and exactly what I was feeling. The hour flew by, and I knew we'd be meeting again the next week, and the next, and the next. Because we'd just broached the subjects, and even though each one could have been its own session, they were so convoluted and connected in my head that I had to just blurt it all out.

I wasn't really good at therapy. I didn't go as often as I needed to, but I figured it was time. And Violet was going now, and that was good. I knew that Violet hadn't been able to deal with being the one who found Allison well and had needed to talk it out. She still did. I knew Harmony had gone to therapy as well, especially after she lost her husband. I didn't know if she went now. It seemed like such a private thing that I didn't want to ask.

I didn't know if I was going to tell anyone that I was in therapy. But I figured maybe I should tell Aiden. Considering that he was going to be a major part of what I talked about. And that was why it was so complicated. He was a major part of a lot of things. A lot of things that I thought and talked about.

It was my day off, and though I had paperwork to do, my brain was a little too full just then.

So I picked up some sushi takeout and headed home,

ready to just veg out and pretend that everything was just fine—even when it wasn't.

I didn't know exactly what I was feeling, but I felt like I was on a precipice ready to take that next step. Would I falter? Or would I actually land on my two feet?

Because I had been telling Mary the truth in my session. I loved Aiden. I just didn't know if I was *in love* with him.

And that was a huge distinction.

As soon as I got home, all four cats came to me, trying to sniff my bag.

"No fish for you. You have food in your bowl, you little lazybones."

All four of them tried to needle, to use those cute little purrs and to bat those lashes on those little eyes of theirs so they could get sushi out of me, but I would not relent.

It was bad enough that I was eating sushi in Colorado, I wasn't going to let my cats eat off my plate while I was there.

I sat at my kitchen bar and snacked on my dinner, ignoring the cats as they tried to jump on the counter for a bite of their own.

When my phone lit up, I looked down at it and smiled.

That had to count for something. Seeing Aiden's name and smiling instinctively?

Maybe I was on the right path.

Aiden: *Just checking in.*

Me: *Just got home. Fighting my cats for my sushi.*

Aiden: *Sounds like life or death.*

Aiden: *Crap. Didn't mean to say it like that.*

It was weird to think how many times all of us used sayings like that, about death and killing and all those little things that meant so much more. But the fact that we were all aware of it in our vernacular had to count for something.

"Just breathe," I whispered to myself.

Me: *It's fine. Seriously. Really. But you should probably know I was at therapy today.*

See? Just rip off that Band-Aid.

Aiden: *You okay?*

I smiled. Damn it. It was going to be hard holding back from this man and protecting my heart. The thing was, I didn't think I had a choice.

Me: *I will be. Hence the therapy.*

There was a moment when I just saw those little bubbles moving, and I wondered what he was going to say.

Aiden: *I'm here if you ever want to talk. I know you didn't before, at least not to me, so I'm glad you're talking to someone. I'm not great with words, I'm really not great* *with texting, but I can be here. Diego too. And I want to try out that dating thing again. I think it's time we tried this right. Without drunk dude-bros.*

I traced his words with my fingers. Did I want more? Did I want to risk everything?

I kind of already was.

And that was the problem.

Because we were already moving down this path. And I didn't think there was any turning back.

Me: *I think a date would be nice. You're working all evening?*

Aiden: *Yeah, just in the stockroom. You should come in tonight.*

Me: *The stockroom you say?*

Aiden: *Yeah, every time I'm in here, I think of your lips. Got to be a good thing.*

I grinned. Oh, sexy talk with Aiden over the phone? In a text? This was new.

Me: *Well, if I get to come down tonight, I might have to visit you in the stockroom.*

Aiden: *And now I'm hard. Thanks.*

I grinned.

Me: *And my work here is done. Be safe with all those knives. Take care of that hand. And I'll try to see you later.*

Aiden: *You suck, short stack. See you soon.*

I grinned as I set down the phone and shooed all the cats away from my food.

This was going to work. I wasn't going to mess this up. We weren't going to mess this up. And I was actually talking. Maybe not to my family, and perhaps not directly to Aiden. But to someone. So, I counted that as a win. Because I wanted to be okay. I might not have all the answers, but I wanted to be able to walk around and not feel scared. I just wanted to work out exactly what I felt for Aiden.

And if I were honest with myself, I wanted to figure out exactly what he felt for me.

Even if it scared me.

CHAPTER TWELVE

AIDEN

I'D ALREADY HAD a day from hell, and I really just wanted a beer and to go to bed. It didn't matter that it was seven o'clock at night and it was my night off, I was just exhausted.

I'd had issues in the kitchen all day, mostly because we were all trying to get back into the swing of things with me actually being able to use my hands, but it wasn't easy when the recipes that I wanted to try out didn't work the way I wanted.

I always joked that I was the best chef out there, but I knew I wasn't. I knew that I was damn good at my job, and sometimes you had to make mistakes in order to figure out what would work on a line as well as on a menu. We'd tried a new appetizer that had ended up taking too many steps since we wanted to start fresh rather than from frozen, and one of our entrees hadn't been ordered with as much as we'd hoped for.

That meant that today hadn't been the easiest of days. I hated the fact that something we tried out didn't work like we wanted it to, and it had wasted time. I didn't cook shit food, I made damn amazing food. But, sometimes, it didn't work for the season and place. So, we learned. We tested. And I spent hours going over how to do my job and still love it. I wasn't in a Michelin-starred restaurant anymore. And while I missed it, I loved my family and my place that was part of my past.

It just wasn't what I used to have, so I figured out how to make it my own. Even if it felt like a step down.

Brendon and Cameron had come in later than I had since they were working the late shift and had growled at each other over one thing or another. Apparently, neither of them had had enough time to spend with their women, so now they were taking their issues of not getting laid out on each other and me.

Dillon wasn't working today since he had school and lots of studying to do. The kid was working on his gen-eds and perhaps a business degree before he decided if he wanted to try culinary school. I'd only had Beckham to lean on, and that wasn't the greatest thing. Especially considering that Beckham tended not to talk and just glowered or made jokes that might have been funny in other situations.

But I hadn't been in the mood for them today.

I had worked the opening shift as well as the early dinner shift, and I was tired. I actually let my sous chef have control of the kitchen and left my brothers to do what they needed to do. That meant I was here alone at my house and tired.

I looked at the little ball of fluff who was trying to look innocent.

Okay, so I wasn't technically alone since this little kitten named Diego was with me and seemed to also be the devil incarnate.

I couldn't believe this little ball of evil contained so much wrath and energy.

Diego seemed to smile at me, then licked his paw and tried to catch his tail all at once. He ended up rolling right off the couch. I moved quickly, grabbing him in one hand and cursing, considering it was my still-healing hand.

"Motherfucker," I muttered under my breath, and Diego looked at me wide-eyed and tried to roll out of my palm before biting my finger.

"Seriously? Seriously?" I brought the cat up to my face and stared at him. "Okay, I'm not really angry at you for destroying the pillow. I shouldn't have left a perfectly good pillow there. I don't even like throw pillows. But, here we are. You are in trouble for tearing it to shreds and for tossing the stuffing everywhere all over my house, though."

Diego tilted his head at me and lifted his back legs so he could bounce them against my thumb like a rabbit. Weirdo.

"Stop looking cute."

Diego let out a little purring mewl, and I narrowed my eyes.

"Stop it. What did I just say?"

Diego licked my thumb, and I closed my eyes.

"I hate you. I hate you."

The little kitten made a little meowing sound that was so high-pitched and adorable, I was pretty sure I would have swooned if I were actually a swooning type of guy.

"What did I say about using your cuteness to get out of trouble?"

Diego just looked at me, his wide eyes innocent yet containing so much evil.

"I can't believe Sienna convinced me to keep you."

Diego just looked at me, his ears twitching.

"Okay, I sort of used you to get into her good graces so I could take her out. But it's not like I've actually been in her pants since then. I didn't use you for completely nefarious purposes."

I shook my head.

"Now I'm talking to a cat. I feel like you're responding to me and answering questions, though that might be because I'm tired. But Sienna says her cats talk to her, so maybe we're all just a little insane. But you're not allowed to tear at my shit anymore. You're not allowed to get cute about it either. Thankfully, you know how to use the litter box, but there's still litter everywhere. It's like it crawls right out of the little litter box and follows you around."

I set Diego down on the cushion beside me and leaned against the back of the couch, letting out a sigh.

"This is ridiculous."

I really wanted that beer, but I was too tired and a little annoyed with myself to get up and get it. Sienna was supposed to come by later and bring a few old things from her cats to my place. We had gotten Diego a couple of toys, but so far, he really only liked to play with my laser pointer, which I didn't use often, and a ball of foil that I had made for him that seemed to be the best toy in the history of toys. I wasn't really sure exactly how that worked, but apparently, foil and boxes were all the rage with kittens.

But there were a couple of old things like beds and mats that her cats hadn't wanted, even though she had bought them, and we were going to see if Diego wanted them. Because maybe if Diego used those to sleep on, I wouldn't have to deal with the cat on my face as I was trying to sleep.

Seriously, the little devil really loved to sleep on my face, my neck, and sometimes with his butt right on my mouth.

That was something I never wanted to feel again.

As I looked down at Diego who was cleaning himself, I was pretty sure it was going to happen again. Often.

Now I was a cat person.

A goddamn cat person.

How in the hell had that happened?

Images of Sienna arching under me as I pushed into her and she wrapped her legs around my waist filled my mind, and then I remembered. Oh, yeah, that was how.

Damn woman.

The doorbell rang, and I froze, looking at the time. She wasn't supposed to be here for another hour. Maybe she'd gotten done with her paperwork early.

"Looks like your favorite person's about to show up," I told the cat and then realized I was talking to the cat and shook my head.

I really needed a dog or something. Or maybe a turtle. A turtle would be nice.

Why the hell was I thinking about getting more pets? I barely had enough time for this kitten, and I already felt bad about that.

I went to the door and opened it and froze.

It wasn't Sienna.

No, it wasn't even close.

I swallowed hard, gripping the edge of the door with my bad hand and holding back a wince.

"Mr. and Mrs. Pritchett," I whispered, my voice hoarse. "I...I didn't know you were coming."

Allison's parents. Allison's freaking parents were at my door. I hadn't seen them since the funeral, hadn't really known what to say to them then, and I sure as fuck didn't know what to say to them now.

I hadn't always gotten along with Allison's mom and dad, but no one really had. They were good parents, but just slightly reserved and a little off-center from everything else. They'd had dreams for their daughter, and Allison had done well for herself, but she hadn't done exactly what her parents wanted, and they hadn't really and truly understood Allison.

They hadn't liked the fact that their daughter was dating some foster kid with a past they weren't too keen on.

But they had never treated me poorly, had never refused Allison wanting to be in a relationship with me.

But they also hadn't been quite welcoming either. I just hadn't known if it was because of me or because that was just how they were.

Maybe that was just how they lived, how they treated everyone. I hadn't been sure, hadn't really known them as well as I probably should have, but now here we were, and I had no idea what to say.

"We didn't know if we should call ahead or let you know we were here, but we took a chance that you might be home." Mr. Pritchett swallowed hard and gave me a nod. "We know you took over your father and mother's bar, and I know that's usually a nighttime thing, but we drove by just in case, and we saw your car, so we stopped by."

I nodded tightly and then took a step back, opening the door a little bit more. "Come on in. Sorry for making you stand on the porch. It was just a surprise." My voice sounded wooden, and I didn't really recognize it. Then again, there was so much tumbling around inside of me, I didn't really know what to feel. These were Allison's parents, and I didn't know what they wanted. I didn't understand why they were here. But I might as well figure it out.

"You have a lovely home," Mrs. Pritchett said as she looked around, clutching her bag to herself. For an instant, I thought maybe she was worried that I was going to rob her or something, but then I saw the pain in her eyes, the stiffness in both of their stances, and I knew this wasn't about me. This was about Allison. I needed to throw away my hang-ups about where I came from, or what they might have thought about me at one point.

Because they were hurting. You could see it clear as day. And if they were hurting, that meant I needed to do something. Or at least be there for them. I hadn't been there for Allison. Not at all.

"Can I get you something to drink? Do you want to take a seat?"

Diego took that moment to prance up to Mrs. Pritchett's leg and sniff at her shoe.

Allison's mom's eyes widened, and she looked down at the little kitten. I held back a curse.

"Sorry about that, he's not really used to people yet," I said, picking him up and pulling him to my chest. "Sienna and I found him on the side of the road, and she already has enough cats, so Diego's mine."

Diego looked at the couple and snuggled into my side as if he belonged there. Apparently, he did.

"Sienna was always good with animals," Mrs. Pritchett said, her voice soft. "Allison..." She trailed off, her voice breaking. She took a deep breath and looked directly in my eyes. "Allison always wanted cats or dogs or something, but she had allergies so we couldn't have pets."

"I remember."

"Yeah, of course, you do." Mr. Pritchett cleared his throat. "We're sorry for coming like this without warning.

We're not very good at figuring out what to do or say these days. It just came as a shock, you know?"

We were standing in my foyer, awkwardly, and I had no idea what to say, so I just spoke.

"It came as a shock to all of us. I hate that. I'm sorry that it was such a shock, and I'm sorry that there was nothing I could do."

"You two hadn't been together for a while," Mrs. Pritchett said, her voice a little steadier. "You were out of her life, and that just means she had other people to rely on. Like she should have relied on us. But we'll never know why she's gone. Probably. We won't know a lot of things. But we're here for a reason, and one day, maybe we can come back and talk about Allison again. But I just wanted to get this over with."

I pulled Diego a little closer, a bit worried about what she was going to say next.

"The girls brought over Allison's things." Mr. Pritchett looked off into the distance before turning back to me. "It's shameful that we weren't strong enough to clean up her apartment ourselves, but we worked on the paperwork and dealt with the sale and everything else. But she was so close to the girls that it felt right at the time for Sienna, Violet, and Harmony to go through Allison's things."

"We were cowards," Mrs. Pritchett put in. She gave

herself a self-deprecating smile and just shook her head. "I think we still are, but we're trying to be better. Trying to understand."

"Sometimes, there isn't any understanding," I put in.

"I think that's what is hard. One of the many things." Mr. Pritchett looked off in the distance again. "But when the girls brought over her things, we went through them. We're still going through them. It's not easy, seeing the aspects of your daughter's life. Parts that we remembered, but also many parts we didn't know." He looked at me then, his chin raised. "We loved our daughter, Aiden. We loved her with everything that we had. Maybe it wasn't enough."

"No, it was enough. I know you loved your daughter. That was never something that was in question," I cut in.

"Maybe. But we'll never know," Mrs. Pritchett said, her eyes filling with tears. She let out a breath. "But as my husband was saying, we went through her things and found something that we think is yours." She reached into her bag and pulled out a little photo, one that made my heart freeze, and the blood in my body go cold. My fingers went numb, and I slowly set Diego down on the floor so I wouldn't accidentally crush him with my fists.

Diego meowed at me and then pranced off to the couch so he could do his thing.

But I didn't really notice, I was just looking at the little black and white photo in Mrs. Pritchett's hand. The image I hadn't known was still around. I had thought Allison had torn it up.

I'd thought it was gone forever.

But there it was, staring me in the face.

A sonogram. With *Little Baby Pritchett-Connolly* written on the bottom.

A baby, a little girl.

A baby that wasn't here anymore.

"We didn't know," Mrs. Pritchett said, tears sliding down her face. She waved the photo just a little, her hand shaking, and I took it from her, careful not to smudge, bend, or do anything to it that could hurt what wasn't there anymore. "We didn't know," she repeated.

"I don't think anyone did," I whispered, my voice hollow. "My brothers don't, and I don't think the girls do either. We didn't tell anyone."

"Will you tell us what happened?" Mr. Pritchett asked, tilting his chin at me.

"If it's too much, you don't have to tell us, but we want to know what happened to our daughter. And that little girl."

"Why don't we take a seat?" I asked, my voice shaky.

Somehow, we all made it to the seating area, with me sitting on the chair in front of the couch where they settled, Diego on my lap. I just looked down at the sonogram and kept it out of reach of the little kitten who wanted to play.

"We were on our way to breaking up when we found out that she was pregnant. It was an accident, but sometimes, accidents are good, you know? We were going to figure out what to do, even if we weren't together anymore. But we were going to try. We wanted to try." I swallowed hard and looked at them. "She miscarried in her second trimester, and she wasn't really showing at all at that point, so no one really knew. We lost the baby, our little girl, and we didn't really talk about it. We just went our separate ways, both of us a little too shattered and scared to do anything about it other than just try and figure out exactly what the fuck was wrong with us." I swallowed hard. "I don't know if that's why she did it. It's been so long, so many years. But I often think about what we could have had. What we lost. Maybe she did, too."

"Don't blame yourself," Mrs. Pritchett put in, her body shaking as she cried silently. "We won't blame ourselves, and you can't either. I hate the phrase that things happen for a reason, but sometimes, things happen for no reason. We didn't know what happened to the child, we thought maybe you both chose not to have one, or you had one, and she went off for adoption, much like you and your brothers."

I shook my head. "No, I think both of us would have

figured out how to be parents. Especially after what my brothers and I went through. We didn't like the system, and I didn't want anything of my blood to be in that system. Even if we were surprised about the baby, we both wanted her, even if we didn't know if we wanted each other anymore. But that was the last straw. We walked away, and then I was around in her life, but not really. I don't know what happened. I do know that we loved that little girl. I think about her every day. I'm just sorry that you had to find out this way."

"We're sorry that you couldn't tell anyone," Mrs. Pritchett said, and then we were silent for a moment, sifting through the memories and the pain of what we had tried to forget, and what we knew we needed to remember.

They sat there a bit longer before I let them out, still clutching the sonogram to myself.

My daughter was gone, never even able to draw her first breath in a world that might have been different if she had been around.

I didn't know why Allison had ended her life. I didn't know anything. I didn't think it was just because of this, though.

Because I hoped to God that she would have found me, talked to me, let me see something.

Though I didn't really know anything.

My body shook, and I set the photo down and just put my head against the door, wondering what the fuck I was going to do.

Because I didn't think I was sad anymore. No, I was just angry.

So goddamn angry.

Then the doorbell rang again, and I opened the door. I knew who it had to be before I even opened it. Sienna stood there, her eyes wide, and her hands full.

And I knew I needed her, I wanted her. I just wanted to forget.

Even if it wasn't the smartest move.

It was the only one.

CHAPTER THIRTEEN

Why are boys so confusing?

-Sienna, age 15.

SIENNA

AIDEN DIDN'T GIVE me a chance to speak before he was tossing the box from my hand to the floor, the resounding crash echoing in the room and scaring Diego off the couch to scurry beneath it.

"What the hell, Aiden?" But that was the only thing I could say. In the next moment, his lips were on mine, and the door was closed behind me.

I didn't know what was up with him, but he was clearly hurting, I could tell. But he didn't want to speak. He just wanted my lips, wanted me.

And this was something I could give him. This was something I wanted, something I needed, too.

So, I let him.

He gripped my ass, lifting me high, so I wrapped my legs around his waist.

"Aiden," I whispered, trying to pull back, trying to breathe. Just trying to collect my thoughts. "What's wrong? Talk to me."

"No talking. Just fucking."

My eyes widened, and then his hand was under my shirt, and my back was pressed to the door, his body grinding against me as he kissed my neck, my jaw, and bit my lips. He did everything, and it was all I could do to just try and hold on and keep up.

Somehow, I caught my breath, but only just.

He kept sucking and licking at my neck, and then taking my mouth, using one hand to prop me up, the other to slide under my t-shirt.

"Aiden," I moaned and then just didn't speak anymore. He wasn't listening, and really, neither was I. Oh, he would listen if I told him to stop, told him no. I knew him. And I knew from the look on his face that he would walk away if I needed him to. But he didn't.

And I didn't want him to.

"You want this?" he growled. "You tell me now, and we're doing this. You want me to walk away? I'm done. You get that?"

I looked at him then, panting. "You mean for the night?" I asked, my voice a bit sharp.

"For the night. Tell me no, and I walk."

"I'm not saying no."

And then he kissed me again, and I moaned.

He had his hand up my shirt, sliding over the softness of my belly and then moving to cup me through my bra. I was wearing a small, lacy number because I had wanted him to see it later, probably much later than just when I walked in the door. But it was happening now, and I could feel the heat of him along my skin through the lace. My nipples pebbled, and he arched into me, pinching my bud through my bra. I bit my lip, trying not to scream.

He pinned me to the wall using his hips of all things and then worked my shirt up over my head before he had his hands back on me, kissing me through my bra, sucking my nipples into his mouth.

"You're so fucking beautiful, Sienna," he whispered, and I blushed.

He'd seen me naked before. We had done this before,

just as hot, just as needy, just as intensely, but he still made me blush.

He set me down on my feet, so that way he could kneel in front of me, kissing his way between my breasts, unlocking the clasp of my bra in front.

My eyes widened as he ripped it off me, and I helped him so I wouldn't dislocate an arm with the straps. His face went between my breasts as he pushed them together, kissing, sucking.

"I could fuck these tits, suck on them all night until your nipples are red little cherries. What do you think about that, Sienna?"

In answer, I let out a little gurgling moan and then rested my head on the door as I ran my hands through his hair. He nipped small bites all over my breasts, and I knew I would have bruises in the morning. I didn't care. I just wanted him.

And so, he kept kissing me, kept sucking, his lips going down my belly until he licked right along the waistband of my jeans, tugging with his teeth.

When his hands went to the button, I knew this was going too fast, but I didn't care. I just wanted him inside me. So, I arched my back just a little so he could pull my jeans over my butt, and then down my legs. I stepped out of them and my shoes and moaned when he kissed me right over my lace panties.

"Pale peach. Good color." And then he shoved my panties to the side and put his mouth on me.

I arched into him, going up on my tiptoes, wanting more of him.

His tongue flicked my clit, and my knees started shaking, but he had one hand on me, keeping me steady, the other moving my panties out of the way more so he could lick and suck and blow warm and cool air on me. And then the hand that was supporting me went away, and he was inside me, two fingers, then three, stretching me and curling ever so slightly so he could find that spot.

I came then, right on his face, and I shuddered, my whole body weakening.

But I didn't have time to breathe, didn't have time to thank him or even scream his name. Because his mouth was still on me, sucking my clit in as he twisted his lips just slightly so I came again, twice in a row, something I had never done before.

Damn, this man.

And then he was on his feet, and I stood there dazed, my whole body pressed to the door. He still had his shirt on, his shoes, but he had shucked his jeans over his ass, his cock hard and ready, and then his hands were on me again, and he was in me.

Just one thrust, hard, needy, and bare.

"Fuck," I whispered to myself.

His eyes were wide. "Fuck. Condom."

"I have an IUD, and I'm clean. I have the paperwork."

"I'm clean too, but I'll get the paperwork. I don't want to move out of you. I can't."

"I trust you," I whispered, hoping I wasn't making a mistake. Then again, I hoped I wasn't making any mistake when it came to Aiden.

He was still in me, his body pulsating against me as he rested his forehead on mine.

"I've never been bare with anyone, I can promise you that."

Not even with Allison? I asked myself. But I didn't say it. Because that name was already between us, it always would be.

"Move, Aiden," I demanded, arching into him.

And then he moved.

Simple thrusts, in and out so he pulled out all the way and then slammed back home, just teasing me, and then moving so quickly, so hard, that I knew we might break his door. And I didn't care.

I clung to him, my nails digging into his skin through his shirt as he pounded into me, needing, aching.

This was raw, powerful, and something primal. So us.

I didn't know if we could ever have soft sex. If we could ever be sweet to each other.

And that was fine. Because this is what we were, just

what we needed.

I needed him. More than I needed anything else in the world. More than I needed any*one* else in the world.

Because right then, it was just the two of us. No other names, no other whispers.

And that's what I craved, what I clung to.

He slid one hand between us, his thumb going over my too swollen clit.

"One more time, short stack. One more time."

I blinked at him, trying to get my thoughts in order. "I can't come. I can't."

"You will." And then he kissed me again, so much in it that I came, his hand still on my clit rubbing so quickly and at such a perfect pace that I shook, my whole body clamping around him.

He let out a groan, and I could feel him come inside me, his body shaking along with mine.

And then it was over, and we were both sweaty, panting, and he was still inside me, bare. I really had no idea what had just happened.

He pressed against me as I slowly cooled, a little embarrassed about what had just happened since he was still dressed, and I was only wearing a scrap of lace that had been pushed to the side.

"Let me get something to clean you up," he growled, his voice hoarse.

I nodded, then winced as he slid out, a little sore. I knew I was going to hurt more in the morning.

It'd been since the last time we slept together that I had done anything like that, but still, we were rougher than I'd ever been before.

He didn't kiss me, didn't do anything, just walked away as he pulled up his pants and tucked himself inside his boxer briefs before he went back to his bedroom. I heard water running, and then he was out again in the living room with two towels in his hands, one damp, the other dry. I felt so open, so bare, even though he had just been inside me, so I slowly wrapped one arm around my breasts, the other covering myself, not knowing why I was so embarrassed.

"Here, let me help," he whispered, and then slid the wet cloth between my legs. I winced, and he froze. "Was I too rough?"

I shook my head. "No, just not used to that. But it's fine. It was good."

He just looked at me, his eyes going dark before he looked back down and finished cleaning me up, then slid my panties back over me.

It was such a strange gesture, one that was caring yet a little off. I had no idea what I was going to say next, no idea what I *could* say. It just felt...different. Like we were different.

I bent down and quickly pulled on my bra, and then my pants. He had my t-shirt in his hands, and I took it from him without saying anything. What was there to say after you fucked someone hard against a door and then it looked like he was embarrassed or a little ashamed of that fact?

"I guess we scared Diego off," I said, trying to lighten the mood.

Aiden just squared his jaw and gave me a tight nod.

"What's wrong, Aiden? Talk to me."

He didn't say anything, just looked down at his hands.

"Talk to me, what's wrong?" I repeated.

"We just had sex, Sienna. What more do you need?" He growled out the words, sounding nothing like himself. I had never heard that voice or tone from him. I had never heard that type of cruelty.

Something was wrong with him, and I wasn't leaving. He would just have to deal with it.

"No, you don't get to do that. What's wrong with you?"

He gave me a casual shrug, and his face went neutral. "I can go again, short stack. Just give me a minute."

And then he moved forward, cupping me between my legs over my jeans. "Unless you want my mouth. I could use a little syrup from my short stack."

There was no humor in his eyes, and I just blinked. I

pushed at his chest, and he took the two steps back, folding his arms over his chest.

"Aiden Connolly. What the fuck is wrong with you? That wasn't a good joke. That was horrendous. What is going through that head of yours? Don't think you can just act like an asshole and push me away. We don't get to do that to each other. You get me?"

"Nothing's wrong."

"No, you're lying. Because you're making cruel jokes and acting like what we did meant nothing when I know it did. So, don't fucking act like this right now. Talk to me."

"I'm fine, Sienna. I don't need to talk about everything."

"Really? Because you're the one who told me I needed to talk about what happened. I'm in therapy for God's sake. And you seemed happy that I was going. But you're not going to talk at all? You're just going to treat me like this? I don't think so. You don't get to just fuck me against the door and then treat me like I'm a whore."

His eyes widened at the word, and then he took another step back before sinking onto the chair. He buried his face in his hands, and I took a couple of steps forward. "Talk to me, Aiden."

"I don't know where to start," he growled.

"Don't treat me like that again, Aiden. That's where you can start."

He looked up then and reached for me. He pulled me onto his lap and buried his head against my chest. I slid my hands through his hair and held him close. "Aiden."

"I'm sorry, Sienna. I was an asshole. I'm always an asshole, but sometimes, I'm worse. I shouldn't have said that. I don't even know why I did. It was stupid. I don't think you're a whore. Seriously. I really don't think you're a whore."

"I didn't really think you thought I was a whore. But you made me feel cheap just then, and I didn't appreciate it."

"I just don't want to talk about anything, so I wanted you out of my house. But I know you're just as stubborn as I am, so you're not going to leave until I tell you."

"I'm not going to pressure you into telling me something you don't want to, but I'm also not going to leave after what just happened. So, we can just sit here and talk about nothing, but I really hope you trust me enough to know that I'm going to be here for you no matter what. So, talk to me." I paused. "Is it about your mom?"

He looked at me then and barked out a laugh.

"Jesus Christ, there's so much wrong with me that it really could have been about just about anything. No, I'm really over my mom. I promise. I've been over her for a while now. Dillon and Cameron and Brendon and I are just fine. It really has nothing to do with them. No, it has more to do with me." And then he looked at me and told me about Allison. Told me about the baby. About why they'd broken up. About it all.

And I just sat there, shaking.

He didn't cry, not a single tear, but I cried. I cried for everything.

I didn't know what to say. Didn't know what to do. So, I cupped his face and lowered my forehead to his. "Aiden."

"I know. Sucks right?" He let out a laugh, and I heard the pain there, the rage. "I don't know what to think. Because it's just too much. It could've been why. It seriously could've been why." He let out a breath. "But what was I supposed to tell everyone? That I thought maybe I knew why Allison killed herself?"

"You don't know that. We don't know anything."

"I know that we lost a baby and we didn't talk about it."

"We can talk about it now if you want." I paused. "Unless you don't want to. I don't want to pry, even though I'm already prying."

Aiden let out a breath again and then looked at me. "I always used to be able to talk to you, Sienna. And even when we fight now, I talk to you. So, it's not that. It's never been that. I knew it was going to be complicated, it's always complicated when it comes to old friends. It just threw me for a loop. Seeing the sonogram, having it all come back to me. I just don't know."

"Her parents know now. So that's something." I paused. "And I think you need to tell your brothers. And maybe the girls, too."

"I do. And we will. I just need some time to myself with it."

I nodded and tried to move off his lap. "Aiden, I can go."

"I meant with you. You know. You know pretty much everything about me now. I don't want you to go." He swallowed hard, and I watched the long lines of his throat work. "I don't want to be alone tonight."

And that was when I fell in love with Aiden Connolly.

Because he asked for help. A man that never did.

I loved him, and I didn't know what to do about it.

So, I just held him and let the tears fall as I thought about my friend who was no longer with us. Thought about everything the two of them had gone through. And then I cried a little bit more about what might happen in the future, and at thoughts of how we would figure out this new normal.

But we would. I had to have faith.

Because without faith in that, I wasn't sure I'd have faith in anything.

CHAPTER FOURTEEN

Sometimes I wish it had been me. But I love her, so
I forget that wish. I have to
   -Sienna, age 17

SIENNA

I ROLLED my shoulders back and smiled at Jefferson. He smiled back, his eyes bright and practically bouncing. Today was one of the good days with Jefferson, so I had to count that as a win. Considering that we hadn't had as many good days as bad days when it came to the former quarterback's therapy for the past month or so, I figured today was going to be a good day all around.

"Okay, you're doing good today. You want to work on the next set?" I asked, putting my hands on my hips so I could take a look around the room to make sure that we had everything prepared. I was still a little off from everything happening all at once, but I was doing better. At least I was able to mask my emotions and exactly what I was thinking from my clients. They didn't need to know that I was still a little shaky from the attack, even though my bruises had long since faded, and I felt physically fine.

They didn't need to know that just thinking Allison's name made me tear up. And now it made me think of Aiden and everything they had lost together.

It hurt to think of everything he had gone through, and how he'd had to hide it because it was so personal between him and Allison. And then losing Allison on top of it all?

No wonder he was angry all the time and constantly pushed others away.

No wonder we always got on each other's nerves, because honestly, we were so much alike sometimes it wasn't even funny.

"I'm ready, Miss Knight. Just tell me where you want me." Jefferson winked, flirting again, and I just shook my head, waving him off. He was having a good day, and he never went too far with his flirting, so I planned to just ignore it. For now.

Jefferson and I got to work, and even though I knew we were both getting tired, we only had a few more minutes together before we could move to the cooldown and he could go home, thankfully with his mother coming to pick him up.

He hadn't missed an appointment in the past month, and I counted that as another win.

I just hated the fact that this was his normal now. And even though we were helping his physical strength in order for him to actually be able to walk without as much pain as he had been in before, some things would never get better.

But there was nothing I could do about that, so I just did my job, something I was actually good at.

We were just finishing up when the door opened, and Aiden strolled in, a smile on his face, and a bag in his hand.

Other than when he had come in for his hand, I didn't think he'd actually ever been to where I worked. He hadn't told me he was coming, and I wasn't really excited that he was here.

Sure I loved looking at him, loved the way he looked at me, but this was work.

And I had no idea how to handle this. I really wasn't good at this.

I made sure the smile on my face wasn't too bright, considering that I was at work, and not only were my coworkers here, but my clients were, as well.

"Hey, short stack," Aiden said as he walked up and kissed me on the cheek. I straightened, taking a step back. I didn't miss the hurt in his eyes or the confusion, but it wasn't like I could tell him to just go away for a minute.

This was where I worked, where I did my best to act professionally in a world where mostly men got the promotions and the respect. I had to work twice as hard, and I knew I even had my own privileges.

I just didn't know how to say that to Aiden just then. I hoped he would understand.

But from the way he looked at me, I didn't think he did.

Because I hadn't told him.

But he should have understood it anyway.

"Hi, Aiden, I didn't know you were coming in."

Jefferson stood behind me, towering over us all, and I held back a wince. This was not something I needed. This wasn't something *any* of us needed.

"Who's this?" Jefferson asked, his voice a growl.

I cleared my throat. "Jefferson, this is my friend Aiden. Why don't you get back to that cooldown, and then we'll work on what we need to do for the next session."

Jefferson just folded his arms over his massive chest. "Not leaving you alone with someone I don't know."

"Excuse me?" Aiden asked, rolling his shoulders back so he looked slightly bigger.

This was definitely not what I needed. Not in the slightest. Now people were looking, and I was the center of attention. Again.

"Aiden, why don't I meet you up front? Jefferson? Go do that cooldown. We're almost done."

I looked at Jefferson. "Please," I pleaded.

"Fine. But I'm watching you." He narrowed his eyes at Aiden and then stomped off to do his cooldown.

"What the hell was that?" Aiden asked, staring after where Jefferson had gone to the mat.

"No, we're not doing this here. Go up to the front, Aiden. I will talk to you later."

"What's wrong?"

"I'm working, Aiden."

"I know, but I figured you had your lunch break coming up like you said, so I brought you your favorite. You know, that curry you like?"

For some reason, that just made me snap. I was tired, and everything was a little too confused in my head. So I said the first thing that came to mind, even though it wasn't the best thing to say. "No, that was Allison's favorite. Don't be like this. Go back to the desk, or just go. I'm working, and I have to be professional. You're not helping anything."

Aiden just looked at me, his face shutting down, He lowered his hand, his gaze hard, then gave me a tight nod and turned on his heel to walk away.

Well, then. That could have gone worse. I could have shot him.

"Everything okay?" Greg asked. I looked at my coworker and nodded, a pleasant smile on my face, even though nothing was going on in my brain right then that made me want to smile.

"I'm doing great. Sorry about that. Unexpected guest. I have to go back to help Jefferson."

"Okay, just want to make sure you're fine. You know... after everything."

I nodded and kept smiling. My perfect, peaceful smile that had nothing to do with the rage and confusion and anger and even a little sadness rushing through my mind just then. Because everybody here knew I had been attacked. They had seen the bruises, had seen the ring around my neck from where that man had held me against the wall. They didn't know I was in therapy, they didn't know that I was dealing with the emotional wind-fall of losing Allison and then hearing about Aiden and

Allison and what they'd lost. They didn't know any of that. But they did know that I had been weak at one point and had been hurt. And now I was trying to act strong and like nothing was wrong, even though everything seemed wrong just then. But I was fine. I was going to be just fine.

"Thank you, Greg. I should probably get back to work." I waved him off and went back to Jefferson. "Okay, Jefferson. How we doing with that cooldown?"

He glared up at me before rising to his feet. I always forgot how tall he was compared to me, about the fact that no matter what happened, I felt like I was always in his shadow. Literally.

"What's wrong? Who was that man? Can I help? Do you need me to pound on him?"

The thing was, coming from another of my football player patients? The comment probably would have been a joke. Jefferson? I didn't know anymore.

With the way that his brain worked now, he could literally go out and find Aiden and beat the shit out of him because he thought that Aiden was trying to hurt me.

And, technically, it wouldn't be Jefferson's fault. Not anymore. It was just how his brain was newly wired because of one too many hits to the helmet.

And it worried me.

Jefferson put his hand on my shoulder, giving it a

squeeze, and looked down at me with an expression I had never seen before.

I swallowed hard and gave him a smile then took a step back.

"I'm fine. But let's work on you, okay? We're almost done today, and then we can work on our next schedule."

There. Perfectly professional. And not creeped out at all. Not worried that I had just fucked things over with Aiden.

Right after I realized that I actually loved him.

Great.

By the time I finished with Jefferson and my next client, I was frazzled and really just wanted a drink. The thing was, I had been planning to go to the bar right after work to see Aiden and the others.

Now, I just wanted to go home. Maybe I would go into the bar later when I wasn't so angry and feeling dejected, but not now.

Now, I didn't know what to do.

When I got home, I shot a quick text to my sister since I wanted to make sure she knew I might not be showing up to the bar and went straight to the freezer for my ice cream.

The cats followed me, Runway sitting on top of the fridge, looking down at me like the empress she was.

I waved at her, and she just huffed, going back to her little nap.

Danger strolled into the kitchen, flicked his tail, and then went to his food bowl. While Moxie and Baby started wrestling right by my ankles. I just shook my head.

"Well, if I fucked things over with Aiden, at least I'll never be alone. I'll have the four of you."

And didn't that just make me want to sob?

I couldn't help but think of Diego, the little kitten who hadn't had much of a chance until Aiden and I had shown up. And then I'd said yes to a date with Aiden to save little Diego's life, even though I knew that no matter what happened, Aiden wouldn't have really used Diego as leverage like that.

But I had wanted to say yes, and Diego had given me an excuse.

And if I had succeeded in pushing Aiden away like I feared I had just then, then that meant Diego would never meet my little clowder of cats.

But I didn't know what to think.

I took out the carton of ice cream, flipped off the lid, and dug a spoon out of the drawer before taking a bite.

"Caramel ripple really does save the world," I said, looking down at my cats.

Yes, I was a cat lady, and I was going insane. But I was

just over everything just then. It was all a little too much. And I didn't really know what to do.

My door opened, and I glared at Violet as she walked in. "So, you just walk in whenever you want to now?" I asked. Violet just rolled her eyes, came into the kitchen, got out a spoon, and took my ice cream from me.

"Hey. That's mine."

"Whine a little louder, don't you," Violet said, closing her eyes and moaning. "Oh, you do have the best ice cream."

"You have the same kind in your freezer." I stole my ice cream back and took another bite.

"True. I always try to keep myself in stock, and Cameron's keeping his freezer in stock for me, too. But your ice cream always tastes better. Probably because I've stolen it from you."

"I hate you."

"No, you don't. You love me. However, let's talk."

"I don't want to."

"Yeah, you do. Talk to me. What is up with you and Aiden?"

"Nothing," I mumbled around my spoon.

"Lie."

"I'm not lying."

"You're totally lying. I will get Harmony and Meadow here right now if I need to."

"No, you don't have to. Plus, I'll see them at the bar later or something."

"So, you *are* going to the bar?"

"I don't know. Maybe."

"Talk to me."

I let out a breath and shook my head. "Some things I can't talk to you about. It's not my place to say."

Violet reached out and squeezed my arm. "Okay. That's fine and perfectly legitimate. If you can't talk about it, then that means it's something going on with Aiden. But I know that face. I know you. Something's going on with you, as well. Talk to me, Sienna."

"I made a mess of things."

"How did you make a mess of things?"

"Aiden came to my office today while I was working, and I got all huffy and told him to leave."

"You were working. You're completely allowed to get huffy if he showed up. I take it he did the normal Aiden thing and didn't tell you ahead of time and just showed up because he was thinking about it?"

"Pretty much. He said he was thinking about me. Which you know, is kind of sweet, but you know me. I have to be professional at my job."

"I totally get you. Cameron doesn't come to my office because I'm a woman in science and as it is, I was already working with my ex-husband's wife. I already had enough of a soap opera at my office. So, we don't add the confusion of him coming there to see what I'm doing while I'm in the lab."

"Though he does go out with you when you go take samples," I mumbled.

"Yes, he does. When it's just the two of us. And it's still a little weird, and I do my best to remain professional." Her cheeks blushed, and I gave her a look.

"Okay, sometimes we go off for a hike when I'm not on the clock and things happen, but you know, that's just natural."

"Getting natural in nature, are we?" I asked, laughing.

"Oh, shut up. But it's different with you. There's a bunch of men at your office, and you have to make sure that you're the perfect professional. One that's not too sexy but not too dowdy either. Not too happy but not too sad. In other words, you just have to be a woman living in this day and age."

"Nail on the head there. And Aiden showed up, and I was a little off. Plus, I always feel off when I'm working with that client." I shook my head. "Nope, not going to talk about that. Not really *allowed* to talk about that."

Violet held up her hand. "Are you safe?"

"I'm completely safe. I just can't talk about anything else."

"Okay. Then I won't ask. But if you ever feel unsafe,

you need to go to Greg or someone. Now, back to what we were talking about. Aiden showed up?"

"He showed up and said he was thinking of me, which is sweet. But it wasn't the right place or the right time."

"And then what happened? Because there's something else. I can tell."

"It's silly," I whispered.

"If you're feeling bad about this, then it's not silly. You have legitimate feelings, and that means something. Talk to me."

"He said he brought me my favorite. Curry. But it isn't my favorite. It was Allison's favorite."

Violet winced and then held out her hands. "Come here."

"Are you talking to me or the ice cream?"

She just glared at me, took the ice cream from me, and stuck it back in the freezer. Then she took my spoon, tossed it into the sink with hers, and then held me close.

"I love you, Sienna. I love you so much. And I know this isn't easy. It isn't easy for any of us. I miss her so much, but with you dating Aiden now, it is a different layer, and I hope you know you can talk to me about it."

I laid my head against her shoulder. "I am talking to you about it," I mumbled.

"Are you talking to your therapist about it?"

I nodded, even though she couldn't see me. I knew she

could at least feel me. "Yeah, I guess I'll talk to her about this, too. But it just annoyed me because he thought he was doing something so sweet, but it was for Allison. And it's not like they've even dated recently. She's not even here, even though she's always here, if you know what I mean."

"I know."

"Of course, you know. It's just stupid. I shouldn't feel jealous, but I do. And then I feel sick that I'm jealous because she's not here. She's not here anymore, and there's nothing we can do about it. And then there's all this other stuff that I can't talk to you about, but I know that Aiden's eventually going to talk to Cameron and then you about it. I may be silly, but I just don't know. It's just a lot, and I can't even breathe sometimes. I just don't know what to do."

"Okay, first thing you're going to do is not blame yourself."

"How can I not?"

"No. You and Aiden are starting this new relationship. You are allowed to do this. It was never hoes before bros with us."

"Because we aren't hoes?"

"That, too. But we've always been conscious enough of our feelings to understand that sometimes we're going to fall. I fell for Cameron again when I didn't think I should. Harmony fell for Brendon, even though Brendon was friends with Moyer. The fact that you and Aiden are together is wonderful. And I do think that Allison would have been fine with it."

"I do, too," I whispered, saying it for the first time. "I think so, too."

"Good. Because Allison was amazing, and she would have understood. You and Aiden need to get through that. He's going to mess up. He's going to mix up silly things like that because it was always the group of us. And, honestly, I thought you liked curry."

I snorted, shaking my head. "Not really. It wasn't my favorite. It was always Allison's favorite."

"But you liked it. Sort of. At least you ate it with us. Maybe that just got confused in Aiden's head because you know...it has been a few years. And he's a chef. He likes cooking, things happen. So, what you're going to do is you're going to go to him, and if he gets all grumpy, you're going to explain to him that when you're at your place of work, there needs to be boundaries and rules. And then you're going to talk about food. Because he loves food, and I know you do too, and you're going to find something that can be yours together and not something that's also mixed up with Allison. But you need to talk with him. Don't do what I did and not talk and then miss out on so much."

"I love you."

She smiled at me. "I know."

"You're not Han Solo," I mumbled.

"Well, he did shoot first, after all," Violet said, rolling her eyes.

And so I laughed and held my sister close. Because I was being silly, and I just needed to talk it out. But that meant I needed to confront Aiden. Which was sometimes my favorite thing, and sometimes made me want to bash my head against the wall.

But hiding from my feelings hadn't helped before, and it wasn't going to help now. So, I just had to do it.

Even if it hurt.

CHAPTER FIFTEEN

AIDEN

I HATED PEOPLE. There, I said it. For a man who owned one-third of a bar and restaurant, that probably wasn't the best thing for me to be thinking.

But my head hurt, and I was just pissed off at the world. So, yeah, I was going to hate people. A lot of people.

I stalked around the kitchen, banging pots and pans and ignoring the worried looks of my staff. They should have been used to my attitude by now. Apparently, I had an anger management issue.

So, fuck everybody. Fuck everybody and their dog.

I paused, wondering why the hell I'd thought that.

I just needed to focus, needed to work, and I needed

to get all thoughts of Sienna and whatever the fuck had happened earlier out of my mind.

I was such a fucking idiot.

I shouldn't have gone to her. Shouldn't have thought I could just take part of an afternoon to see what she was up to.

And I probably should have brought her the right fucking meal instead of what I'd thought I remembered was her favorite. No, I'd just made a colossal mistake and brought Allison's favorite meal instead of Sienna's. Could I be any more of an idiot?

I honestly hadn't meant to make that mistake. I'd thought I was on the right track. I'd truly thought that curry was what she liked to eat. But instead, I had mixed her favorite up with Allison's, just cementing the fact that I wasn't good at relationships. I wasn't good at anything. Except for cooking. I could do that. I was a goddamn chef, and I was going to act like it.

And that meant being quirky was fine. Because Sienna expected that of me.

"Hey, there're people out here looking for you," Beckham said, leaning against the doorway.

"I'm not in the mood to deal with people," I growled.

"Don't really care. They're out here, and they asked if you were here, and I said yes. So, be a good little boy and go talk with them."

I glared. "Shut up."

"Oh, yes, that's a great comeback. But, come on, you can take five minutes before the big rush starts and talk to these people. They said they met you at a hockey game or something." I pinched the bridge of my nose. Oh, good. People I had to talk to. I couldn't wait.

"We've got it, Aiden. You've been in such a mood that you've been faster than usual getting everything done. Just let us take over for a minute."

I glared at my staff and then shucked off my apron and put it on the hook. "Fine."

"And if you act like a petulant child any more, I think I'm going to have one of your brothers slap you," Beckham said. I flipped him off then sucked in a deep breath and let it out slowly. "Sorry. I'm in a mood."

"You don't say."

"How has no one ever punched you before?" I asked.

"No one wants to hurt this pretty face," Beckham said with a wink, although something did pass over his eyes when he said it. I wondered what the hell that meant. But I had my own problems, and the fact that Beckham was sometimes a broody asshole and sometimes a sarcastic one wasn't something I could deal with right then. He acted like the rest of us, so I couldn't really blame him.

I walked out to the bar where Olivia and Derek were sitting, Derek tilted to the side, so Olivia's chair was right between his legs. They were looking at each other as if they were the only two people in the world, and I couldn't help but feel a stab of jealousy.

I didn't remember when I had decided that I wanted that with Sienna, but it'd just happened. We just had this thing, and then it'd turned into me wanting her in my life. But I couldn't pinpoint the exact moment when. Should I be able to?

I didn't know. Maybe that was part of the problem. But I looked at the way Derek and Olivia were with each other, and I realized I wanted that. Yes, I wanted that, but maybe Sienna didn't. Perhaps I was the one who wanted too much. Just like before. After all, I'd had to use a kitten to get Sienna to date me. Maybe I wasn't good at this. I already knew that she was better than I was, and she was slumming it to be with me, but I hadn't known it would hurt like this.

But I was getting ahead of myself. I would just push that away and talk to these two.

"Hey. You came," I said, clearing my throat.

"It's a nice place," Olivia said, smiling.

"You mentioned it, and we thought we'd stop by. But you're probably getting busy. You don't have to be out here too long."

"No, I have a few minutes."

Beckham chuckled under his breath and went back to

cleaning the glasses. I flipped him off discreetly under the bar. Apparently, not discreetly enough since Derek started laughing.

"No, really, the place is great. I think we came in here before. I don't know, maybe a year ago or so, I'm not quite sure. It has the same vibe as before, but maybe a little different?"

I swallowed hard and just smiled. Business. I could do this. "Yeah, when our dad passed away, the bar came to us. We've changed a few things but tried to keep it what it's always been, the Connolly Brewery."

"I'm so sorry," Olivia said quickly, reaching out to grip my hand tightly for a moment before letting go.

"Yeah, sorry. Didn't mean to bring that up. The two of us know better than anyone what it means to try and move on and pick yourself up after you lose someone close." The two of them shared a look that was so private and filled with pain yet hope that I felt like I was intruding. I didn't ask what they were talking about, but I nodded. "Thanks, we're doing okay. We're figuring things out. But the fact that the place is getting busier is a good thing."

"Tell me about it." Derek just shook his head. "Restaurants keep popping up all over the place down here, and then they fade away just as quickly. I'm glad this place is staying, though. You're only a couple streets down from my shop."

"Which is a good thing, considering I'm still thinking about what my next tattoo should be."

"We're here for you whenever you need us, but we gotta put your name on the waiting list."

Olivia bounced in her seat. "He's full-time now and actually has a waiting list instead of just walk-ins. It's a big deal." Olivia did a little booty shake in her seat, and Derek just rolled his eyes.

"Yeah, it's a big deal, but the shop and its name kind of helps with that."

"And probably your talent, too," I said.

"Speaking of talent, we're getting those nachos that I've heard so much about, and the people next to us had when we first walked in. They look and sound delicious."

"Then I should probably get back and make sure I make them for you personally."

"Oh, you don't have to." Olivia shook her head quickly. "I mean, we'd love you to, but if you have other things to do, just do your thing. We're just here. We just wanted to say hi and thank you for dealing with us at the game. We were sad that you left early."

I sighed. "Those assholes in front of us got a little handsy."

"We know," Olivia said quickly. I gave her a look, and she just smiled. "Sienna and I exchanged numbers, and I texted her to make sure that she was okay since you guys didn't come back, and we didn't hear from you. That's why I didn't ask right when we walked in how things went. But I'm glad you're both okay, and I'm glad we're here. I think Sienna said she might be stopping by later, too, right?"

I tried not to stiffen at the sound of Sienna's name or mention of any plans she might've had. I just nodded. "She comes in often with her sister and friends. Two of them are dating my brothers, so they tend to come here often."

"All in the family?" Derek asked. I just laughed.

"Apparently. Let me get to the back and help out with those nachos for you, and then I have some other things to do. But it was good to see you. I'm sure Sienna will see you guys if she comes in, too."

"No problem. Thank you," Derek said. I nodded at them before walking away.

Well, it seemed that Sienna had made fast friends, and I did like the pair. I didn't venture out of my circle that often, considering I had just been in my kitchen before, only worrying about that and trying to move higher up in the ranks. I didn't have time for friends. I hadn't had time for my brothers either.

But then everything had changed, and now my life revolved around the bar, my family, and Sienna.

I just didn't know what to do about that.

I worked up the nachos for Olivia and Derek, then handed them to Beckham directly so I could get back to work since we were getting busier.

Cameron was behind the bar with Beckham, while Dillon and Brendon were on the floor, keeping everything lively and on track.

Dillon could've been back here with me, but since we were a little busy, it was good to just focus and not have to worry about teaching. Not that I resented that, not in the slightest, but sometimes it took a little too long to train when I didn't have that time.

Another hour passed, and I rolled my shoulders back as Beckham came in with an empty tray.

"Hey, it's slowing a bit, and the brothers need you out front."

He passed me without waiting for an answer. I just shrugged and handed over my kitchen to my staff before going out to the front. I might be the head chef, but I was also part owner, so I had to deal with more than just the back. Even though that might be exactly where I wanted to be for the night.

"Hey, what's up?" I asked, keeping the growl out of my voice as much as possible. I was still on edge, cranky, and all I wanted to do was figure out what the fuck was going on with Sienna. But now was not the time.

"We're slowing down since it's only Thursday and

there's no game on tonight, so I figured you could have a taste of this new beer I got."

I blinked. "We're working. I'm not going to drink on duty."

"You can have a sip because you're not going back to that kitchen tonight. You aren't on duty anymore. Your shift ends now."

I folded my hands over my chest. "Excuse me?"

"You weren't supposed to work tonight anyway. Remember? You were supposed to take the night off and work with me on inventory and maybe even taste the beers."

I shook my head. "No, that's tomorrow."

"Yeah, because I was going to let us all have the night off on a Friday."

I tried to think of my calendar and then shook my head.

"I'm really having an off day it seems."

"Yes, you are. So, have a beer, taste it with me. And then let's talk."

I looked down at Dillon, who was sitting at the end of the bar with his textbooks in front of him and a glass of milk. I couldn't help but smirk.

"Milk, young one?"

Dillon flipped me off without letting anyone see him. I just laughed.

"Beckham's the one that poured it for me. I could have gone with like a soda or something or even water. But no, I get milk."

"And as soon as your balls drop and you get that chest hair you've always been wanting, you'll be able to get something other than milk," Beckham said with a wink as he went back to help another customer.

"He's getting better with those zingers," Cameron said, smiling.

"I agree. Thankfully, it's only with us and not the rest of the staff."

"Well, he's an asshole, but he's our asshole," Brendon said.

"I feel like that needs to be the family tagline," Dillon said, laughing.

"Yeah, well, that might be right."

I sighed and went to one of the back tables where we could all sit. It had been slowing down, and that meant I could take some time off and let my staff do what they needed to do. Considering that no one had told me that I had said I was taking the day off just meant that they were used to my moods. I didn't know how I felt about that, but I was head chef. It was sort of what I did.

All three of my brothers came and sat down next to me, Brendon helping Dillon with his books while Dillon carefully brought over his glass of milk while rolling his eyes.

"Oh, good, don't waste the milk."

"Yes, apparently, it's good for my bones."

"And we want you to keep growing, little one," Cameron said, pinching Dillon's cheek.

"The family love here is just so much, it's making me want to throw up," I said, laughing.

"Good to see you laugh," Cameron said, leaning into me.

"So, what the fuck's going on with you?"

"What do you mean?"

"You're in a huff, you forgot that you weren't going to actually work in the kitchen today, and you keep acting like you're a bear with something in its paw."

"I am not."

"You are, too," Brendon said.

"Is it Sienna?" Dillon asked, looking straight at me.

"I have no idea what you're talking about."

"It's Sienna," all three of them said at once, looking at each other and not me.

I hated them. I really did. And the fact that Dillon fit in with us so well, just said that he was indeed a Connolly and we were all fucked.

Or maybe we were just a family, and everybody was

happy, and I just needed to get over myself. But...whatever.

"Everything's fine."

"Lie," Brendon said, sipping his beer. He looked up at Cameron and tilted his head. "Good. Not too hoppy. Nice and refreshing. Maybe this should just be a seasonal one, though?"

Cameron nodded, taking another sip of his. "I agree. Something a little more limited so that way it drives up the sale. And something we can taste some more. I don't know if it's going to fit into our regular stock."

"Seriously?" Dillon asked, looking between us. "You're going to talk about beer instead of the fact that Aiden is stressing out over Sienna?"

"Beer's important, it's kind of our livelihood," Cameron said, his eyes filled with laughter.

"No, food is our livelihood," I snapped.

"Okay, so food is your livelihood, that's great. What's wrong with you and Sienna?" Dillon asked, throwing his hands up into the air and almost spilling his milk.

"Women are complicated."

"Well, that's an understatement," Cameron muttered.

"Well, if you ask me..." Dillon began.

"No one asked you," I snapped.

"Listen to the kid," Beckham said as he dropped off a plate of nachos that I did not make but still looked really good. "Seems like the only one of you who knows what he's doing when it comes to women, or at least talking about them." He winked and then went off to go do whatever the fuck he was doing.

"I hate him," I muttered.

"No, you don't. Now, why don't you tell us what's wrong with Sienna? Or what you did to make things wrong with Sienna," Dillon corrected.

"Fuck all y'all." I sighed and then told them exactly what had happened. Brendon and Cameron just kept shaking their heads, and Dillon gave me such a disappointed look that I felt like I needed to cower in my seat.

"What?"

"She was working, Aiden."

"I know. And I realize it was stupid. I just didn't realize it at the time. I thought she could take a break. Like I do."

"But she doesn't walk back to your kitchen and talk to you. She waits 'til you come out here. Plus, the whole food thing."

I shook my head. "Okay, that was wrong. I just... I can't... I don't know what I'm doing."

"Start with that," Dillon said, tapping his fingers on the table. "Tell her you don't know what you're doing. That way, you can actually figure out what you need to do together. Relationships are hard."

"I still don't know where you're getting all this information," Cameron said, tossing his hands up into the air. "How and why do you know things like this?"

"Like I said, I read romance novels. I watch TV. I listen to women."

"What women?"

"Your women," Dillon said, rolling his eyes.

"If you actually listen to what they're saying, sometimes, you can figure out what you need to do. Or if you don't know, you ask."

"Seriously?" I asked as I shook my head and then pointed at Dillon. "I don't know what I'm going to do about Sienna, but one day, you are going to meet the woman of your dreams, and you're going to freak out and try not to fuck it up. And then you're going to come to us not knowing what you're supposed to do, and we're going to just throw back all of your advice to you. So, it'd better work."

"Oh, it will work. But I'm not coming to you for advice."

I just glared. "Really? We're your big brothers. Who are you supposed to go to?"

"I'm going to your women," Dillon said, like it was the most rational thing in the world. It didn't mean that it *wasn't* the most rational thing in the world, but still. "They're better at this than you guys are."

"He is not wrong there," Brendon said, nodding.

"I hate all of you."

They just gave me a sad look, and I nodded, knowing I had been in the wrong. But that didn't mean I knew what I needed to do next. As soon as the door opened and I looked up, I knew my time for mulling it over and trying to figure out what to say and do was over.

Sienna stood there, her face set in straight lines, and her chin raised.

The time of my reckoning was here.

I just hoped I didn't fuck it up.

CHAPTER SIXTEEN

Don't forget to say what you mean and don't back down

-Sienna, age 19 in a conversation with Violet about her grades.

SIENNA

I DIDN'T HAVE to wait long at the door before Aiden was pushing Brendon out of the booth and coming towards me. I knew I looked stern and ready for anything, but I was literally shaking in my shoes.

I didn't want to lose him, I didn't want to mess this up, but I was still so pissed off.

We got angry with each other all the time, we liked yelling at each other. It was our thing. But it was our thing when the yelling didn't matter, and it just led us to the next step of whatever we were doing.

When the words mattered, when they hurt, that was when I got scared. Because what if we messed up? What if we were wrong?

What if we couldn't fix this?

I took a step back out of the doorway, and suddenly Aiden was right there in front of me, the front door to the place closing behind him. He cupped my face and kissed me hard, his lips pressed firmly to mine. I couldn't catch my breath, and I almost fell into him. Instead, I put my hands around his forearms and held on, letting his tongue touch mine, letting myself feel every inch of him.

"I'm sorry," he rushed out, leaning his head against mine. "I'm so damn sorry."

"Okay, that's a good start. But I had a whole diatribe I was going to go through. Can you let me do that?" I didn't like how flustered I sounded, but at least we were on the right track. Maybe.

He nodded and let my face go, but slid his hands down my shoulders and arms to grip my hands.

"This isn't how it's going to work. Okay?"

His eyes shuttered. "You mean us?"

"Not exactly. We are working great. I'm not breaking up with you." I said the last part fast, and he just nodded.

"Good, because I'm not breaking up with you either." He nodded again.

That made me laugh. "Okay, good. We really need to get better at this communication thing."

"I know we do. My brothers tell me that often. Especially Dillon."

"Dillon's the sage one."

"So he thinks."

"But we're getting off track here. I was working, Aiden. I don't own my own place, and I have to be professional. Plus, these guys trust me to touch their bodies and be professional. I can't flirt with some random dude in front of them."

He narrowed his eyes. "I'm not random."

"Oh, fuck off, Aiden. You are random to them. Get over yourself and see what I mean."

He tightened his jaw but nodded at me. "I know. I shouldn't have shown up like that. I should have waited in the hallway, or at least seen when you had time off. I'm sorry. But I wanted to see you. And I'm not good at this whole thing. You know that. You've known me forever."

"I do know that. But we need to figure out how to make this work for us and not just pile things on top of everything that we had in the past. Because we aren't those people anymore. We aren't the people that we were when we knew each other so well. We've had time apart, and that means we're different people now."

"And I like the person you've become."

That made me smile.

"Well, good. However, while I like the person that *you've* become, we also need to figure out how we fit into each other's lives now. And that means if we want to see each other, maybe we shouldn't just show up at each other's places of business."

I winced and looked up at the bar I was standing in front of. "Well, if we do, then maybe not go to where we're actually working. I mean, I can be standing in front of your bar, and that's fine."

"I get you. Like you don't come into my kitchen, and I won't go back to where you're actually working with clients. But if I want to stop by and you're busy, I'll leave a note or something."

"Or text me. I might not have my phone on me all the time, but I want to see you. And I know our schedules don't always work, and sometimes you're working late, or I need to get up early, but we're going to make this work. 'Cause I want to do this. We're doing this. And you don't get to get all huffy if I need to be at work."

"Fine. And I wasn't huffy."

"You definitely huffed. You huffed and stormed out,

and then I had to deal with everything at work after."

He cupped my face and sighed, kissing me softly.

"I'm sorry about that. I won't do it again. It was stupid, I just wanted to see you, and I didn't think about anything else. It's just been a long time since that sort of thing happened. And I'm not good at this."

"Well, we're going to get good at this."

"Sienna?"

"Yeah?"

"I'm sorry about the food. I thought you liked it before. I was wrong."

"I liked it because Allison did," I said honestly. And then I leaned into his chest for a hug before pulling back. "We're very complicated, so yeah, it's going to hurt sometimes. We'll figure out exactly what my favorite food of yours is so that you can bring it to me. Or you can bring a variety of things as long as you don't think it's my favorite because it was Allison's."

"Yeah, that was a mistake on my part."

"And I probably shouldn't have been so harsh about it when you brought it. But it was just one thing on top of another."

"We'll figure it out."

"Just don't push me out and walk out like you did again, okay?"

"I can't promise that. My temper gets the best of me

sometimes. I'm trying to do better about it, but I'm not great about it."

I kissed him again.

"Maybe we need to talk about that, too."

"I was never good at therapy."

"I'm not good at it either, but maybe it'll help."

"And then we can talk."

"Maybe."

He kissed me hard and then smiled against my lips. "You know I'm at work."

I pushed at him, laughing. "You're outside of your work. But if it's a problem, I won't kiss you."

"Kiss me all you want. I kind of own the place. And I know it's completely different than your place of business and how things work. I'm not going to be that asshole again."

"Thank you."

"I noticed that you're not contradicting the fact that I said I was an asshole."

"The first step in fixing a problem is realizing you have one."

"Sure, whatever you say. You know, the guys kinda kicked me off the job for the night. Do you want me to take you home?"

"I took the light rail in, so that would be nice."

"Let me grab my things."

He kissed me again, and I sighed into him, hoping this would work. Because I loved him. I loved him so much that it was scary. But I wasn't ready to tell him. That time would come. We just needed to work out the kinks in the first part of our relationship. And then we could get to the whole love and future thing.

"Do you want me to stay over tonight?" Aiden asked as we got into his car.

"That would be nice. But what about Diego?"

He cursed under his breath. "I suck at remembering him. I mean, not really, because I'm not a horrible cat parent. But I'm not good at the spur of the moment things."

"Well," I squeezed his hand, "if we're going to keep seeing each other, and if we ever spend the night at each other's houses, we're going to have to worry about the cats. So, maybe we should bring Diego over to my place." I winced as I said it, and Aiden gave me a look of mock horror.

"I don't know about their safety."

"What do you mean, their safety?"

"I worry about your four cats."

"Diego's a little tiny ball of fur."

"He is Satan. Satan himself."

"That kitten is not Satan."

"I don't know. If I call him Satan, he comes running

right to me."

I laughed, shaking my head. "You cannot call that kitten Satan, Aiden Connolly."

"Satan is as Satan does."

"That is not the same, you weirdo."

"I can't help it if he's demonically possessed."

"He's not demonically possessed. He's just in that kitten stage."

"And when does that kitten stage end? Is it going to be anytime soon?"

"Well, I think maybe three or four years."

"Dear God."

"Well, I mean, the kid stage lasts like eighteen years, and then you have to deal with them as adults, so I guess cats are better than humans in that way, right?"

"You say that, but then when you have kids, you're going to have to deal with them *and* your cats."

I swallowed hard, purposely not looking at him when he was talking about kids. Because we were so not ready for that. Just because I loved him didn't mean we needed to talk about kids right then.

"Well, if that ever comes up, I'll deal with it then. But first, we can try to introduce Diego to my cats. They're actually pretty accepting of other animals, most of them anyway, I just have to be careful about not actually owning the five at once by myself."

"Okay, we'll bring over little Satan."

"Aiden."

"Fine. We'll bring over the baby not Satan, but if he tries to eat your cats, we'll lock him in one of the bedrooms. Preferably one with padded walls."

"You never want to give something with claws a padded room. He'll shred it."

"Okay, cement walls. And chains. Lots and lots of chains."

"I never knew you had such a torture side."

"Well, Satan brings it out in me."

"Diego. His name is Diego."

"You say Diego, I say Satan. Tomato, tomahto. We should have named him Diablo."

"You're ridiculous."

"You haven't had to deal with Satan."

"I have four cats. I think I can deal with your kitten."

"Famous last words."

Diego was excited to get in his little carrier and buckled into the backseat, and we even picked up a couple of things for Aiden so he had something to wear in the morning. I noticed that we didn't pack him any pajamas, and I was just fine with that. I didn't think we would be needing them.

"Okay, are you ready?" I asked, looking over at him. He had his bag over his shoulder, and little Diego clutched tightly to his chest. We had taken him out of the carrier because he was so small that it should be fine. Okay, we really took him out of the carrier because he was adorable, and we couldn't help it. But, still. Adorable. I opened the door and looked back at Aiden. "Wait right there. Just let me see if the cats notice."

I closed the door behind him, and we stood in the foyer as the four cats slowly made their way into the living room. Oh, they knew something was amiss. They knew that there was a stranger. And it wasn't Aiden.

Runway walked right up to me, looked behind me at Aiden, huffed, and then flicked her tail at me before walking away.

That was a good sign. She didn't growl, she didn't hiss, but I was probably going to have to figure out exactly what she would do later.

She walked back to the couch and sat on it, glaring.

The boys came at me, both of them glaring.

Diego let out a little mewling sound, and I winced.

Of course, he wanted to announce his presence. There were big cats here, and he wanted to play.

"He's wiggling, Sienna," Aiden whispered.

"Oh, just be careful."

I tried to sing-song it, but I was a little worried. Moxie looked right up at the kitten, his eyes wide. Then he dashed out of the room, scared to death.

"Is that very large cat scared of this kitten?"

"He's afraid of his own shadow sometimes. It happens."

Danger went right up to Aiden, rubbed his body all over his legs, and sat down, looking up at Diego.

"Okay, bend down slowly and see if they want to sniff each other."

"And leave my hands in the way of claws?" Aiden asked.

"Perhaps."

He slowly knelt down in front of Danger, and Danger sniffed at Diego while Diego lifted his little paw and patted Danger on the face. But there were no claws. I counted that as a win. And then Danger licked Diego's face and sauntered away.

"Well, he's claimed now," I whispered, holding back the laughter.

"So, this is going good then?"

I winced. "Just wait for it."

And then Baby came in. She ran from the stairs and slid across the hardwood floor before catching her feet and running towards us. Diego was still in Aiden's hands, crouched, but at the commotion, Diego bit Aiden's hand. Aiden let go. Diego was on the ground, and we were both trying to catch him, but then suddenly, Baby was on top of Diego, and they were rolling around, screaming at each other and yelling. But no claws, and no teeth. They were just playing.

Aiden reached in to try to grab one of them, but I pulled him back.

"No, let's not get you bit." He held up his hand. "He's lucky he didn't break the skin already," he said, shaking his fist.

"Well, I think Diego's made a friend." Danger and Baby started rolling around with Diego, playing and pulling at each other's tails but not playing too roughly. Moxie watched from the sidelines as if he wanted to play but was still a little too scared.

Runway, however, flicked her tail as she passed all of them, ignoring them as she walked to the bathroom. Then she slammed the door in front of us, and Aiden blinked.

"Well, I'm going to have to pay for that later," I said, shaking my head.

"Did she just throw a tantrum and slam the door?"

"She does that when she wants space. However, Baby knows how to open the door, so it's a whole thing. It's why she had food and water and her litter box in there. Sometimes, she just wants her space."

"They're like people. With personalities."

"Well, yes, they tend to do that."

Okay, I think the cats are doing fine, but let's hang out in the living room with them for a bit."

"Okay, but I still fear for your cats' lives."

"I don't know, Baby can probably take them all."

"I'm going to put my money on Diego." And then he kissed me hard, and I leaned into him. This felt good. Right. Like I wasn't making mistake after mistake.

So, I sat with my boyfriend on the couch and just cuddled into him, kissing him every once in a while, letting his hands roam over me as our cats wore themselves out before falling into a puddle—at least the four of them with Runway still in the bathroom—and I figured that was a good sign. If the cats could get along, and Aiden and I could talk to each other, maybe that meant this was the next step. Perhaps this could be a sign of the future. But I didn't want to think too big, so I let Aiden's lips trail along my neck, and I arched into him, just wanting to hold him. Just wanting to be with him.

Because this was a step, one I had to treasure. And I remembered that not everyone had these steps. Not everybody made it this long.

So, I wasn't going to forget how blessed I was.

Wasn't going to forget everything that had happened.

But I would try to forget for just a moment. And just be.

Because it was time.

Finally.

CHAPTER SEVENTEEN

AIDEN

I WOKE UP, finding myself unable to breathe. I tried to inhale and then coughed, fur in my throat. I tried to shake my head a bit, but whatever was on top of me rolled slightly so it was now on my eye. Oh, great. I was dying. Smothered by a cat.

There was a giggle beside me, and I reached out and tried to grab Sienna, only to come up with very soft flesh. So, I gave it a squeeze.

"Really? That's how you're going to wake me up?" Sienna asked, laughing.

"Well, can't help it, you're nice and soft and all plump and ready. But the cat is on my face. Which cat is it?"

"Well, if it was any cat other than Diego, you probably

wouldn't be able to breathe at all right now. But you guys are so cute. Look at my boys," she sing-songed. I heard the click of her phone camera.

"Are you taking a photo right now?"

"Yep. And I know that since you're not actually forcing the cat off you, you like him just as much as I do."

"I'm afraid if I push him off me, he's going to claw my eye out or something. Sienna, get him off me."

"Aw, look how you whine." But she did reach out and grab the kitten, pulling him up to her very naked chest.

"Okay, you have a kitten on your boobs."

She glared at me. "He's on my shoulder, not actually on my boobs. But I was naked. But then so are you, and then the cat was here. I don't usually sleep naked, so I'm not used to having the cats try to sleep on me. They usually just take over the end of the bed." She gestured towards the foot of the bed, and I looked at the fact that there were indeed four cats in various napping positions lying on the comforter.

"No wonder you have a king-sized bed."

"Well, I can barely fit by myself with these four cats. And now with you and this little kitten? I'm going to need a California king I think."

I shook my head. "I have a king at home too, though I don't know why."

"Well, if I ever bring my clowder over, you'll know why."

I shuddered. "Maybe I'll just sleep here for the time being." She smiled at me, and I realized what I'd said. As if this would be a very future thing and would always happen. I couldn't help but like that. A lot. I looked at her then, noticing the way her hair fell over her breasts and how she laughed at the fact that Diego was now trying to knead Danger's back. She was amazing. A light. A goddess. And while I may have had a crush on her when we were younger, it was nothing compared to what I felt for her now. And it was weird because we had done our best to stay away from each other, to forget that we had been a part of each other for so long. This had just happened. And, yes, when I looked at her, I still saw the bruises even though they weren't there anymore. I still saw what had finally pulled us together, an attack that never should've happened. But I saw the strength beneath that, too. I saw the woman that I cared about. The woman that cared about me. She made me happy. And that meant I just had to keep doing the right thing and not mess things up because, as was evidenced by what had happened the day before, I was really good at messing things up.

"Wait, did you really take a photo of me while I was naked?" I asked, looking up at her.

She blushed. "Yes, but the blanket's covering you. There is some naked chest, but damn, Aiden, you have a very beautiful naked chest." She winked, and I rolled my eyes then reached out and cupped her breast, flicking her nipple between my thumb and my forefinger.

"You have a very lovely chest, as well." And then I froze and looked down at the five cats who I swore were looking at me. "Um. Maybe we can kick them out?"

She looked over and winced. "Yeah, I've never actually had sex in this bed before other than with myself, and even then, the cats aren't allowed. So, yeah, maybe we can go take a shower and see what we can do there."

I was still reeling over the fact that she had never had sex in this bed other than with herself. I swallowed hard. "So, you masturbate a lot in here then?"

She blushed, all the way down to her very flushed nipples. "Well, does every day count as a lot?"

I choked on my own spit and sat up quickly, looking down at the now-tense area of my crotch. "Well, I mean I do it every day too, so I hope it's not a lot or we probably have a problem." I swallowed hard. "Though I haven't actually done it in a while because, well, I've been with you, and you know I'm not as young as I used to be."

She laughed at that and reached over to kiss me gently. Then Diego moved between us, and we both scattered back, laughing.

"I haven't actually made myself come often without you around recently either. But I guess that can change if you want. But the cats need to be away first." She winked and then rolled herself off the bed, dancing naked towards the bathroom. I looked at the cats, who all looked at me with suspicious gazes, and shrugged. "Well, I'm going to go follow your mother, and we're not going to talk about what's going on. Okay?" I asked. I realized I was talking to cats but, apparently, I was a cat guy now. It's just what happened. So, I rolled off the bed and also walked naked towards the bathroom, closing the door behind me. I laughed along with Sienna as we looked down at the little cat paws pushing their way under the bottom of the door, followed by little meows. "You really have no time alone, do you?" I asked, pressing my body against her and kissing her hard. My dick slid between us, pushing against her belly, and her breasts felt perfect against my chest, her nipples hard little points that I could actually feel.

"You're pretty damn amazing," I whispered, kissing her again.

"Well, you're pretty amazing, too. And, no, I never have time alone. They're always like that. Apparently, it's the same with kids." I looked at her then, imagining her round with my child, and then imagining us raising him or her. I swallowed hard, trying not to think too far into the future. But then I just couldn't help it, she was right there.

"I never really wanted kids before. I don't really know if I want them now." She looked at me then, confusion on her face, but not hurt. I held my breath, trying not to say too much or think too hard.

"I wasn't asking to have your baby," she said casually. I shook my head, "Well, I didn't think you were, but I'm just saying I didn't really think about it before because I didn't want to think about it. With my mom and how the foster system was, it just wasn't something on my mind. And then it had to be on my mind when Allison and I got pregnant, so I just want you to know that I don't know what that part of my future is for me. I had to think about it once, and then I forced myself to never think about it again."

She cupped my face then and kissed me softly on the chin.

"It's okay, Aiden. We're pretty new at this. We're allowed to take our time. And we don't have to actually talk about children or what we want in our futures yet."

"But I don't want to lead you down the wrong path where you want kids and then suddenly I don't know if I do or not."

"Aiden, we've only been on a few dates."

"That doesn't matter. We're not just some normal couple. We're Aiden and Sienna."

"I know. And that's why I'm actually having this

conversation with you naked in my bathroom while my cats try to get in. Let's just take it one step at a time. We'll figure out what we want. Because I don't know if I want kids either. I have a lot of cats as it is. But we can make that decision later. First, we have to make sure that we're exactly what we want. And that's going to take time. Right?" I watched her eyes search my face and then nodded.

"Time." I cleared my throat. And then kissed her again.

"Speaking of time, I know you have to get to work soon, so I better be quick." And then I went to my knees and made sure she woke up exactly the way we both wanted. With her in my mouth, and frankly, in my heart.

CHAPTER EIGHTEEN

Happiness isn't easy. Just keep at it
  -Sienna, age 14 to her brother, Mace, after he had been dumped.

SIENNA

I WAS STILL BUZZING by the time I got to work, smiling at everybody and just enjoying myself. I was pretty sure I had a sign on my face somewhere that said, *Just got laid.* But it was fine with me.

Because I was happy. Aiden and I were working

things out. My work was going well. Everything was going great. Yes, that meant things would probably fall apart at any moment, but I was fine with that theory because I was just going to live in the moment and enjoy the bliss.

It helped that Aiden had made me come three times that morning and I was still a little sore where it counted, but that was fine with me.

Because I got some. I got some. I got some.

I was only working a half-day today since my hours weren't always consistent depending on my players' schedules. That worked for me because that meant I could go and finish some paperwork and head down to the bar later to see how I could help the men there because it was Friday night, and I knew they would likely be busier than usual. That was great for them, and I was so glad that the bar was doing better. That also meant that I had a place to hang out with my boyfriend.

My boyfriend.

Aiden Connolly was my boyfriend.

And maybe later I would write his name in my notebook and put little hearts around it, little rainbows and circles.

"You okay over there?" Rocko asked, smiling at me.

I looked up at the offensive lineman and just grinned.

"I am doing wonderful."

"New boyfriend then, Miss Knight?" He winked.

I rolled my shoulders back and glared at him. "I can have a wonderful day without a man in my life."

"Oh, you totally can. And I know you do. You're one of the best ones here at what you do. However, that glow on you? That's love."

I looked at Rocko.

"You're not supposed to actually notice things like that."

"Hey, my wife has been training me how to act around women and to see their moods since I was sixteen. I still sometimes miss when she gets a new pair of shoes or a different haircut, even though it looks like the exact same haircut she had before, but I try. However, I can read that mood, and that happiness comes from love."

"You're far too observant. And we need to be talking about your progress and not my love life."

"But you have a love life, so praise be. And I'm sure my wife will be happy to hear that."

I froze, looking at my paperwork. "Why on earth would your wife be happy about that?" Suddenly all these thoughts of his wife worrying that I was working with him and other things swamped me. Mostly because one of my other clients when I first started had had a very possessive wife who had tried to get me kicked out of the practice because she hadn't liked my hands on her husband. The guy hadn't minded, but since the wife had, I had moved on to different patients. Maybe I would have made a different decision now, but when I was starting out? I hadn't wanted to deal with hurt feelings or anything that could get me fired.

Rocko quickly shook his head, his hands up. "Maddy likes you. You're always nice to her when she comes in. And you answer her questions since I'm not the best at making sure I can help her figure out exactly what's going on with me, or how to say it. Maddy just wants to see you married. She wants to see everybody married." He grinned then. "She wants to see everyone pregnant, too. It kind of helps that we're having one of our own."

That made me smile and push all thoughts of whatever had happened before out of my head.

"You're having a baby?"

"Took seven years of us trying and getting different fertility treatments and stuff, and it didn't help that I wasn't feeling up to it all the time if you know what I mean."

I held up my hands. "You don't need to explain further."

"Hey, you're sort of my doctor. You know what kind of meds they put me on and all that stuff. But, anyway, we are finally having a baby, and she is going to be here in about three months."

"Wow, you really are along then."

"Yeah, we didn't want to say anything until she was really showing and we were out of the woods for that first set of worries. It's not easy, you know?"

I thought about Allison losing the baby and how devastated Aiden still looked when he thought about it. He would always be devastated. Frankly, so was I. My best friends had lost their daughter, and there was nothing I could do about it.

"I know. Well, if there's anything you need, like trying to work around your schedule with the new baby or something, let me know."

"Thanks. I figured Maddy's going to come in a bit once we figure things out, and we'll see what I can do at home. Because I want to be at home more now with the baby and helping Maddy. But I also don't want to mess up my back along the way. Or my neck."

"Well, we will figure out exactly what we need to do. But you're allowed to lift a couple of pounds."

"Yeah, that's true. But Maddy's worried I'm not going to be able to lift her if something happens to her, you know?"

That was a real fear because his spine did have issues, something that we all needed to think about.

"Okay, so we'll figure out exactly what we need to do. But let's finish you up here, and then Maddy and you can come in, and we'll figure out exactly what steps you need to take in case something happens. But we're going to go with the idea that it's not going to happen and we'll just take safety measures."

"Sounds like a plan, Miss Knight."

I smiled then and went back to work. By the time I was done with him, my own shoulder had started to ache, so I did some stretching exercises and went back to my office. Jefferson was standing in the waiting room, talking to the front desk clerk when I passed. I frowned. I didn't think he had an appointment today, but since he wasn't paying attention to me, I went back to my office to go and check. I should be done for the day, so it was a little weird that he was here, but maybe he had an appointment with someone else? No, that didn't make sense. Perhaps I'd just forgotten.

I went to my tablet and looked. He wasn't on the schedule. He wasn't even on the schedule for next week, in fact.

Weird.

I picked up my things, stuffed them into my bag, and walked out to the front area. Jefferson wasn't there.

"Hey, Sandy, why was Jefferson here?"

"Oh, he had a question about getting to see you this week, but I said that you were full."

"Really? Is something wrong?"

"No. Honestly, it sounded like he just wanted to see

you. He said that nothing was wrong. He just wanted extra time. But you're booked, and you're past overtime hours if you add him in."

"Well, if he calls again, maybe I can work something out."

"Okay, I'll let you know. But you know Jefferson. Sometimes, he just likes to have extra appointments with you."

"I know."

"You know you can talk to Greg if it gets weird."

"It's not weird yet. But I'm very aware of it."

It seemed that everybody had noticed that Jefferson had a crush on me, and that wasn't good. I'd told Aiden that I needed to remain professional, but that meant that my patients had to be professional, as well.

"You know what, I'll talk to Greg tomorrow."

"Jefferson's a sweet man, but he's also a big guy and can make you uncomfortable."

"I know. It just annoys me that I feel uncomfortable at all. But this isn't the time or place to talk about it. I'll figure out exactly what I want to say, and I'll talk with Greg later."

"Okay, girl. You have a good day, and tell Aiden hi for me." She waved at me after she'd said it.

"I swear. Am I wearing a sandwich board that says something?"

"No, honey, you're wearing a smile. One that reaches your eyes in the most perfect way. I'm happy for you."

I tightened the strap on my bag and smiled. "I'm happy, too."

I made my way out to my car and lifted my head up to the sun as it beat on my face. It was nice not having to work the full day so I could actually enjoy some of it. Yes, I needed to do some paperwork, but I'd been working a little too many hours back to back lately, trying to make sure that I kept up with my caseload.

But I was having a good day. A really good day.

I had just reached my car when someone put their hands around my throat and tugged my ponytail. I didn't have my keys out, didn't even have the little cat thing that hadn't saved me before.

Flashes of the man's hands on my throat from before and the feeling of brick behind my back and against my cheek slid into me, and I froze. I didn't fight. I didn't do anything. I needed to fight. What was going on?

"Why don't you see me?" the deep voice rasped in my ear. I knew that voice.

I sucked in a breath, trying to breathe. But I couldn't.

He was squeezing my airway, tugging me back towards the bushes.

He couldn't take me to a secondary location. I knew that from all of the stupid podcasts and TV shows that I watched and listened to. So, I kicked out, using whatever strength I had to try and scratch him.

I kicked back into his knee, and he let me go. I fell down to the cement, the gravel of the parking lot digging into my palms. I crawled forward, trying to get to my feet and looked around at Jefferson, who glared at me.

"Why can't you see me? I left you the roses. I left you everything. Those men hurt you, and all I want to do is say I love you and I want to be with you, but you don't want to be with me. Why do you keep doing this?" He slammed his fist into his head, moaning over and over again. But there was no one around to hear. No one around to do anything.

What was Jefferson talking about? The roses?

Then I remembered. I hadn't asked my neighbors about them. I'd just assumed that they were from them. Just like the pies and the cakes and things that had actually been from them.

Oh my God, I was so stupid. I was so worried about everything else that I hadn't really thought about what was going on.

"Jefferson. Jefferson."

I was standing then, my palms out. I knew blood was dripping from the cuts there. My throat hurt, and I knew tears streamed down my cheeks, but I didn't know what to do. He was so much faster than I was.

"You had to go out with him. With that asshole. He doesn't even know you. *I* know you." He slammed his fist against his chest a few times. "I've always loved you, Sienna. Why don't you see me?"

"I see you, Jefferson. Everything's fine."

"Nothing is fine. Nothing will be fine again." Then he came at me once more. I turned around quickly, but he tugged on my ponytail again. I hit the ground, and then he hit me. One time. Another. I curled myself into a ball, trying to protect my face, but he just kept hitting me. I screamed, and then there were voices, shouts, but I couldn't hear them, not really.

It was like I was in a tunnel. Everything hurt.

Everything hurt so much.

And then there was nothing.

CHAPTER NINETEEN

AIDEN

I KNEW DANCING while chopping was probably not
the best thing in the world to do, but I was still doing a
little hip shake as I chopped onions.

I had come in early from my shift so I could go
through some paperwork with Brendon, and then figured
I would help with some of the prep before I went back to
help Cameron with inventory. I was just filling in and felt
good knowing that I had some really good staff members
who knew what they were doing. I knew I needed to hire
another line cook, and that would come. But first, I would
just enjoy my day. I had woken up with a cat on my face,
but I'd had some amazing sex and had most likely taken

the next step in my relationship with Sienna. I was just happy.

It had been too damn long since I had felt like this.

And from the way everyone kept looking at me, yeah, they knew it, too. I wasn't acting like myself. I wasn't being an asshole.

Maybe this was a good thing.

I was humming to myself as Cameron came running into the kitchen, sliding on the floor, gripping the edge of the wall to steady himself.

I dropped my knife and glared at him. "What the fuck is wrong with you? You do not run in here. We have knives and oil."

"It's Sienna. You need to come."

My stomach dropped to my feet, and I was already walking towards Cameron, untying my apron and tossing it at one of my staff members.

"Someone take care of my kitchen."

"We got it, chef. Take care of your girl."

I didn't even know who'd said it. I couldn't pay attention.

I trusted my people. I had trained them. They could handle it.

But Sienna needed to be okay. What was going on?

Images of her attackers came to mind, and I almost threw up.

"What's wrong? What's happening?"

"I don't know. Violet just called and said Sienna was attacked in a parking lot. At work."

I looked at Cameron, rage pushing through me, and I forced myself not to make fists at my sides or punch something.

I wanted to yell. I wanted to scream. I wanted to rip someone apart.

But that wasn't going to help anyone.

I just looked at my brother and tried to calm my breathing.

"At work? You think it was those guys?"

Bile coated my tongue, but Cameron shook his head.

"No, Violet made sure to tell me that. But we need to get there, and then maybe they can tell us everything."

"Is she okay?" I stopped where I was and gripped Cameron's arm so hard I knew I was going to leave bruises. Cameron put his hand on my shoulder and looked at me.

"You're fine. She's fine. She's going to be okay. She's a little banged up, at least that's what Violet said. We just need to get there, okay? She's alive, Aiden."

I looked at the face that was identical to my own. It told me that the fear that was on that face was the same as mine, just a little different.

I couldn't breathe, couldn't focus. But then hands were on my back, and Brendon was pushing me towards the door, Dillon opening it, keys in his hand as he jostled from foot to foot.

"Come on, we've got to go."

"I got the bar. You take care of our girl," Beckham called, and I looked over my shoulder. Beckham slid off his jacket. He wasn't even supposed to be here this early, none of us really were. But somehow, we were all there. And we were going to get through this together.

But dear God, Sienna had to be okay. She had to be fucking okay.

I sat in the front seat as Dillon drove us, and Brendon and Cameron got into Brendon's car. Apparently, they thought it would be best to have more than one car in case someone needed to leave.

I didn't know how they were all thinking so clearly when all I wanted to do was throw up or punch something. But there was nothing I could do. Everything was out of my hands. It was Allison all over again. We were losing the baby. I was losing her. Everything was just going wrong, and I couldn't fix it.

I put my head in my hands and tried to control my breathing.

Dillon let go of his death grip on the steering wheel

and reached out to pat my shoulder. "She's strong. She'll be okay."

I looked at him then, my breaths coming in ragged pants. "She shouldn't have to be strong. I wasn't there. Again."

"You can't be there for her all the time, Aiden. She was at work. It's daylight."

"And she was attacked. Again. This is fucking Denver. This doesn't happen here."

"It happens everywhere. But she's fine. And we're going to figure out what happened. But you need to calm down. They're not going to let you stay in the waiting room if you break through the drywall or something with your fists. You need to act calm and rational and try to figure this out, okay?" There was fear in Dillon's voice, and while he usually sounded older than he was, I could hear the child there. Hear the fact that he was scared, too.

And I remembered that Dillon had dealt with our mother longer than I had. And now our mom was dead, and I didn't know if Dillon had been there when it happened. I didn't know anything about that connection because I chose to ignore it. But I wouldn't from now on. I would ask if Dillon wanted to talk about it.

But right now, I just nodded at my little brother. I was thankful that he was here, even though he was just as scared as I was. Because I could hear it. I could see it on his face.

Somehow, Dillon got us to the emergency room while obeying all the traffic laws and without getting us into a car accident. Cameron and Brendon parked a few spaces away from us, and we all jogged towards the emergency room.

Harmony and Meadow and Violet were standing in the waiting room, all huddled together as we walked in.

The women looked up, and then tears slid down Violet's face as she ran to Cameron's side. My brother held her close, murmuring in her ear as Harmony went up to Brendon and wrapped her arms around his chest. They all held each other, and Dillon and I just looked at Meadow, who gave us a soft smile.

"We're waiting. We're waiting for news. I was with Violet when I heard, so I came." She swallowed hard, and I reached out and gripped her shoulder.

"Thanks."

"Yeah. I'm going to go actually head to the bar now and help Beckham out because I think he'll be short-staffed. And I know this needs to be a family thing. But you guys just keep me in the loop, okay?"

I frowned as she walked away and then looked at Dillon.

"What was that about?" Dillon asked. I shook my

head. I had seen the fear in her eyes, and I figured there was a reason she didn't want to be here, didn't want to be in this hospital after what had happened. And that was fine. She could have her secrets, but I wasn't really thinking about that right then. I was just thinking about Sienna. About Sienna and the fact that we didn't have any news.

"What can you tell us?" I asked Violet, keeping my voice calm. Collected. Because even though I wanted to hit something and I wanted to rage, I thought about Sienna at that hockey game and her pale face when I got angry. And it calmed me down. Because I didn't want to be that angry man. I didn't want to be the person that put fear on Sienna's face. I didn't want to be the one that made her remember what had happened in that alley.

And I sure as hell didn't want to be the person that reminded her of what had just happened today.

Fuck, this was too much.

"Apparently, one of the people that she works with, one of her clients, there was something wrong with him or something. I don't really know, but he came at her in the parking lot and just kept hitting her. They know she tried to fight back because they could see it on her hand or something. I don't really know. But he knocked her out, and now they're doing a concussion protocol. She has a few stitches from where she hit the pavement or something. I don't know. I don't know anything." She started shaking, and Cameron held her close before sitting down in one of the chairs and pulling her onto his lap. He kissed her forehead and just whispered to her as I looked at Harmony and Brendon, who were holding each other, the two of them pale but steady.

I looked at Dillon, who was wiping tears from his face before he went and sat down next to Cameron, taking Violet's hand in his.

We were a family. It had taken way too long to get here, to get to the point where we could rely on each other like this, like we should have done the whole time.

But we were here.

And my stomach hurt.

I just wanted to see Sienna.

"Are you the family of Miss Knight?" one of the nurses asked, and we all stood up, shaking.

"We're her family," Violet said. "All of us are."

"Our parents and my brother and his family are on their way. But we're all family here."

The nurse looked at us and didn't even flinch at the idea that all of us were one big family. Because we were. Blood didn't change that. We were a family.

"Okay, then. Miss Knight is awake, and she's doing okay. She's a little banged up, and we're going to keep her overnight to monitor her concussion. She has some bruising, and some stitches. But she's going to be just fine. There's no doubt in my mind that she is going to recover a hundred percent very soon. Now, only two people are allowed back there at a time, so you're going to have to take turns."

I looked over at Violet and gestured. "You and Cameron first. And then the rest of you. I'll go last."

Violet gave me a weird look. "Are you sure, Aiden?"

"No, you go first. I'll be her last. Because you're not going to be able to pry me out of there without a crowbar." That made Violet smile, and I knew it was a real one.

I waited with the others while Violet and Cameron went first, and then Harmony and Brendon. Sienna's parents showed up next, giving everyone hugs and kisses before going in. And then Mace and Adrienne came, the big brother of the girls looking dour and big and all tattooed and broody. They hadn't brought their daughter, and for that I was grateful.

All of us had had to deal with a little too much recently, and none of us wanted a little girl to have to deal with that. She was staying with Adrienne's family down in Colorado Springs, so that was good.

And then it was my and Dillon's turn. Dillon had offered to wait even later, but I knew he wanted to see her, even for a minute.

So, we walked in, and I had to sit near the doorway,

doing my best not to stress out. I hadn't asked anybody what they'd seen, what she had said. Number one, that was for them. But mostly, I didn't want to know. I didn't want to think about that while I was waiting.

"Hey, you two," she said, smiling, looking so strong.

I saw the bruises around her neck again, the ones on her face, the cuts and abrasions on her skin. Her beautiful, beautiful skin, cut up and bruised with some stitches on her arm and on her chin.

That asshole had hurt her. I could barely breathe.

"I'm so sorry," Dillon said and leaned forward to kiss her softly on the lips.

I raised a brow and looked at the kid, who shrugged.

"She's my sister."

"Okay."

Dillon took a seat next to her and took her hand, just laying his head on the bed, his whole body shaking.

I took a few steps towards them both, meeting Sienna's gaze, and then put my hand on the kid's shoulders. "You're okay. We're all okay. She's fine."

"I can't lose any of you guys, okay?" Dillon said, sounding far younger than he was.

Sienna moved to reach out and touch him, but then winced, and I shook my head. "She's fine. She probably just needs some sleep. Why don't you come back a bit later, okay? She's fine."

Dillon stood up then, wiped his tears, kissed her on the forehead, and then hugged me tight around the middle. I wasn't expecting it, so I took a few steps back and kissed the top of his head. He was almost my height, but because Dillon was leaning slightly, I could do it.

"I want to go and feed all the cats. Well, I need your house key, but I'll get it from Violet, okay? I'll take care of everything."

He waved and then jogged off, and I wondered how that had just happened.

"I forget that he's a kid sometimes. Even at eighteen. He seems so much older."

I looked at Sienna then and sank down into the chair Dillon had just vacated.

"I forget, too. And I missed out on so many of those years. All of them, really."

"You're not missing them now."

I tasted salt on my tongue and realized I was crying, so I leaned forward and took her lips. Softly so I wouldn't brush any of her bruises. The fact that it was hard to do broke me.

"Sienna."

"It's fine. I'm fine. I'm just really tired of being in this hospital."

"I never want to see you bruised again."

"I have cats. I run into walls. I'm going to get bruised."

"But not like this. I don't want this to ever happen to you again. I don't think I can stomach it."

"I don't want to stomach it either. I want to be okay. They arrested him."

"I don't want to talk about him." I growled out the words, but she didn't flinch. I told myself I had to calm down. Because she was already pale enough, and I didn't need to see the fear on her face like I had at the hockey game.

"He had a traumatic brain injury, Aiden. So he had a lot of issues. Always had. And he sort of fixated on me, I guess. I don't really know, and I figure we'll hear more about it later. But after my attack in the alley, I think it sort of triggered something in him. Like he thought I was his and he hadn't been able to protect me."

I laughed, but there was nothing funny about what she'd said. "I thought the same thing. That it was my fault that you had been hurt. That I should have been there to protect you."

"Yes. So it's a normal, common thing. But if you already have a brain injury, sometimes, it can mess things up for you. And it messed him up. I don't think I can blame him," she said, her voice hard. "I *want* to blame him. I want to get angry that I'm in this hospital bed again and that my whole body hurts and that I'm afraid, but I can't. Because you can't really blame someone who can't help or think for themselves."

"You don't have to blame, but I might blame a little bit. I'm pretty sure your brother or my brothers are going to want to blame a lot, too."

"Fair enough. I just don't think I have it in me right now."

"You don't have to do anything. You just have to heal. I'll take care of you."

"And I might just let you."

"I was so scared. I was so scared that I would never be able to talk to you again. Never see you. I didn't realize how important you were to me until I realized that no matter what happened, I wanted you in my life."

"I'm fine, Aiden." Tears filled her eyes, and I shook my head, leaning forward so we were nose-to-nose.

"I almost lost you," I growled out, trying to stay calm. "I love you, dammit. I don't want anything to happen to you."

Her eyes widened some, and then she smiled. "I love you too, Aiden. I don't want anything to happen either. So let's just try to live in the moment like we said we'd do, okay? Because I love you so much." I wiped her tears from her face and kissed her softly, trying not to touch her stitches.

"I didn't realize I loved you until I thought I'd lost you.

Not really. And shame on me. Because I should have realized what those feelings I was having were."

"I'm kind of new to them, too. I didn't realize until I almost lost you before either."

"At your work?" She nodded. "You wouldn't have lost me then. I'm an asshole, but I wasn't that dumb."

"Well, sometimes we're dumb together. Now, can you just sit here a bit longer and talk to me about food or something silly?"

"There's nothing silly about food," I said, and she laughed before wincing.

"Okay, maybe not something funny. Maybe just something calm. I just want to hear your voice. And I just want to be with you."

"Then can we yell and fight with each other later?"

"Of course," she said softly. "I hear the makeup sex is the best part."

"That's the Sienna I love and adore."

"Can you say it again?"

"That I love you?" She nodded. "I love you, Sienna Knight. I didn't really understand what that word meant when I was a kid. I didn't understand that you could have a family who loved you, that you could have people in your life that you cared for that were part of your soul. And while I loved someone else, someone close to us, it wasn't the same. I hope you realize that. I hope you know that you're my everything. My it. I'm going to do every-thing in my power to make sure that I'm worthy of that, okay?"

She was crying again, and I wiped her tears one more time. "I loved her too, Aiden. She'll always be here between us. But that's okay. Because she should be. We should never forget. I'm so glad I get to love you. I'm so glad that I get to call you mine. Even if it hurts a little."

My heart thudded just a bit, and then I nodded, wiping away my own tear. "I think we can do that. I think that's the perfect way to honor her. Although, if you tell anyone that I'm crying like this, I will have to take away your favorite foods."

"Deal. We'll both be stern and strong and not cry." She hiccupped a sob, and I kissed her again.

"I love you, Sienna," I whispered.

"I love you, Aiden Connolly. Even if I hated you first."

And then I laughed and held her hand, wanting to hold the woman I loved but knowing that she needed to heal first.

Because it had taken us too long to get here, even if it felt like a blink.

And though I wanted to punch something, wanted to scream at the world for what had happened, I wasn't going to. Because she was my touchstone, my calm in the storm.

And I would never take that for granted. Never again. Sienna Knight was mine.

And I would do everything in my power until the end of my days to let the rest of the world know that, so they understood.

EPILOGUE

I love you. Always.
-Sienna, today.

SIENNA

"I REALLY WANT A BEER," I said, leaning against Aiden's chest.

"You had your last painkiller this morning. Meaning tomorrow, you can have a beer. Today, you're just going to cuddle with me and use me as your liquor."

"That was a horrible line," Brendon put in. "Like a *horrible* line."

"I can't help it, I'm cheesy now. It's a thing." I laughed against Aiden, but I didn't wince this time, so I counted that as a win. It had been a week since the attack, and things were getting back to normal. Whatever normal was.

The attack in the alley when I had been mugged was a one and done thing, something I would probably never get answers to, much like a lot of things in my life it seemed. But we hadn't been able to find the attackers, and I didn't think we ever would.

I was finally going to take another set of self-defense courses, but that didn't start for another two weeks. I still had to heal. Putting it off before because I had been busy was stupid. And it'd almost cost me my life. I never wanted to be that person again.

Jefferson was facing charges of assault, but not attempted murder. He didn't even have to face stalking charges because those wouldn't do anything to him anyway. And while I didn't blame him fully for what had happened, I knew he needed help. And physical therapy wasn't enough for him. He needed help beyond that, maybe even seeing a therapist every week.

He needed help that I couldn't give him, and honestly, the thought of being near him again scared me.

So, he was no longer my client.

I didn't think he was really going to serve time, but he was likely going to be admitted somewhere for help.

And maybe that was the silver lining in this. Because he needed help. I just hated the fact that it had taken what it had for him to get some.

"So, like whose turn is it next?" Violet asked, snuggling into Cameron's side.

I looked around at the bar, confused. We were pretty busy, and the fact that I just said *we* meant how much I thought of the Connolly Brewery as my own. But considering it was a weeknight and the rest of the staff was working, it wasn't too bad. I still didn't know what Violet had meant.

"Huh?" I asked.

"Well, Cameron and I are together, Brendon and Harmony are together, and now you and Aiden are nice and sweet and have that lovey-dovey face. Who's next? Dillon?" We all looked at each other and then up at the bar where Dillon was wiping it down before going to bus tables.

"I think he needs a little more time, don't you think?" I asked Aiden.

He shrugged. "I think that kid's probably better at understanding women than any of us. Women excluded, of course."

"You know, one day, he's going to get knocked on his butt, and he's not going to see what hit him," Cameron said.

"And I can't wait for that," Brendon said, and the three men clinked beer glasses while us women just rolled our eyes.

"I think next should be your bartender," Harmony said before kissing Brendon's cheek.

"Beckham?" Brendon scoffed. "He's going to have to stop brooding and making fun of us if he wants to actually settle down."

I met Violet's gaze and then Harmony's, and we just smiled at each other as the guys looked confused.

Oh, we had an inkling of when and who Beckham might settle down with. It was just going to take time. And lots of planning.

But we could do that. We had time. And Beckham deserved a happily ever after.

And so did a certain friend of ours.

But tonight was just about us.

The Connolly brothers were officially in the deep black when it came to the bar. Violet's new paper was being published. Harmony had gotten a huge check for her charity, and I was going back to work next week.

Our lives had all taken separate paths from each

other, maybe when they shouldn't have, but the worst had brought us together.

And though none of us would ever be fully over that, the fact that we could find love even in the darkness was something that I would never, ever forget. It was something that I would treasure always.

"I love you guys," I said quickly, wiping away a tear. Aiden looked down at me and frowned.

"You okay, short stack?"

I flushed at that, because every time he said "short stack" now, I thought of something dirty. Thank you, Aiden Connolly.

"I'm fine. Just thinking about why we're all here together again. You know, what started it all."

The mood dampened just slightly, and then Aiden cleared his throat and held up his beer.

"To Allison. One of us. No matter what."

I held up my water glass, and the rest of them held up their beers, and we clinked glasses and toasted the woman who had been a part of us. The one who was no longer here.

I missed her with every breath I took.

And I hoped she was happy wherever she was. I hoped she wasn't in pain anymore, if that had been the reason for her leaving us.

But Allison's death had brought us together, and that

was something that I would have in my heart for a long, long time.

I had found my calling, had found my trust in my sister and my best friend.

I had made new friends, new connections, even through the fractured pieces.

I missed Allison, I knew we all did, but none of us were as broken as we had been when we first lost her. And we could say her name and toast to her without breaking down now.

Perhaps that was a blessing, a next step. I wasn't sure, but as I sank into the hold of the man I loved, I figured we all had our own paths to follow, our own futures to pave. And through it all, we would have one person by our side, even if she was no longer with us.

Because she had brought us together with her passing.

I loved every single person at this table, and I knew they would be there for me no matter what.

And that was something worth falling for.

THE END

The Fractured Connections series continues with Taken With You.
Don't miss the other books in the series, Breaking Without You and Shouldn't Have You.

www.CarrieAnnRyan.com

A NOTE FROM CARRIE ANN RYAN

Thank you so much for reading **FALLING WITH YOU.** I do hope if you liked this story, that you would please leave a review! Reviews help authors *and* readers.

This series is heavy, I know that, but in the end, there is hope, there is that happily ever after. I wanted to write a series where there is love even when it doesn't feel like there can be.

I'm honored you're reading this series and I do hope you continue on. This is possibly one of my most personal series and I'm blessed in the fact I get to write it.

Meadow and Beckham surprised me and screamed that they needed their stories as well, so their story is coming in Taken With You!

Did you see Derek and Olivia? They're from Inked

Nights! Want to know what those blushes were about? Read their story!

Will I write Dillon's story? Just wait and see!

If you missed Cameron and Violet's story, it's called Breaking Without You and out now! And Brendon and Harmony's story is Shouldn't Have You.

BTW, in case you didn't know, Mace and Adrienne had their story in Fallen Ink as the Fractured Series is part of the Montgomery Ink world!

And if you're new to my books, you can start anywhere within the my interconnected series and catch up! Each book is a stand alone, so jump around!

Don't miss out on the Montgomery Ink World!

- Montgomery Ink (The Denver Montgomerys)
- Montgomery Ink: Colorado Springs (The Colorado Springs Montgomery Cousins)
- Montgomery Ink: Boulder (The Boulder Montgomery Cousins)
- Gallagher Brothers (Jake's Brothers from Ink Enduring)
- Whiskey and Lies (Tabby's Brothers from Ink Exposed)
- Fractured Connections (Mace's sisters from Fallen Ink)

- Less Than (Dimitri's siblings from Restless Ink)

If you want to make sure you know what's coming next from me, you can sign up for my newsletter at www. CarrieAnnRyan.com; follow me on twitter at @CarrieAnnRyan, or like my Facebook page. I also have a Facebook Fan Club where we have trivia, chats, and other goodies. You guys are the reason I get to do what I do and I thank you.

Make sure you're signed up for my MAILING LIST so you can know when the next releases are available as well as find giveaways and FREE READS.

Happy Reading!

The Fractured Connections Series:
A Montgomery Ink Spin Off Series
Book 1: Breaking Without You
Book 2: Shouldn't Have You
Book 3: Falling With You
Book 4: Taken With You

Want to keep up to date with the next Carrie Ann Ryan Release? Receive Text Alerts easily!
Text CARRIE to 24587

ABOUT THE AUTHOR

Carrie Ann Ryan is the New York Times and USA Today bestselling author of contemporary, paranormal, and young adult romance. Her works include the Montgomery Ink, Redwood Pack, Fractured Connections, and Elements of Five series, which have sold over 3.0 million books worldwide. She started writing while in graduate school for her advanced degree in chemistry and hasn't stopped since. Carrie Ann has written over seventy-five novels and novellas with more in the works. When she's not losing herself in her emotional and action-packed worlds, she's reading as much as she can while wrangling her clowder of cats who have more followers than she does.

www.CarrieAnnRyan.com